BRIDE BY MISTAKE

by

SERENITY WOODS

DEDICATION

To Tony & Chris, my Kiwi boys.

CONTENTS

Chapter One

After eighteen years of absence, Fliss was finally going home.

Strange how she thought of the Northland of New Zealand as home when she had no ties to the place anymore. She lived in LA now, and even though her family remained in New Zealand, they resided in Wellington, so she'd had no cause to return to where she'd been born. It had hardly featured in her thoughts at all. Why would it, when she'd traveled to amazing cities like New York, London, and Paris? Even most New Zealanders thought of the Northland as a backwater, the jewel of the Bay of Islands a great place for a holiday, but rural nonetheless. And yet now, as the plane's wheels touched down, tears rushed into her eyes.

Maybe that was more her state of mind, though, than the thought of returning to her childhood home. She hadn't even gone to Wellington to visit her folks this time; she'd flown straight from LA to Auckland to Kerikeri. It offered a refuge from the madness of the real world, from the cameras and the gossip columns, from Facebook and Twitter and Instagram. Here she could take off the mask that was Felicity Rivers the actress and just be Fliss, the girl who used to walk barefoot to school, and who swam in the river in her underwear before she was old enough to care what boys thought.

Was that girl still there? Or had she disappeared beneath the weight of press attention, the way a life raft would submerge if pulled down by too many grasping hands?

The plane taxied up the runway and came to a stop in front of the Bay of Islands terminal. Some things don't change, she thought, looking at the tiny building and the guys unloading the luggage—no conveyor belt here, just a trolley that would be wheeled into the room with the bags once the passengers had disembarked. She was half-surprised that she hadn't gone to board the plane and found a sign on the door that said, "Flight cancelled; out fishing." It had often been the case that the Northland shut down when the weather was fine.

A small crowd waited in the tiny arrivals area. As Fliss descended the stairs, she saw people waving at family and friends, some crying, others beaming huge smiles as they threw their arms around loved ones. She slid her sunglasses on and walked with her head down into the small arrivals lounge, then stood at the back of the room. Nobody even looked her way. It was amazing how the public never gave her a second glance when she went out on her own. It was as if she had to put on a mask and flick on an internal switch to become Felicity Rivers, and when the switch was off, everyone ignored her. She'd once read that Marilyn Monroe had been the same. It was said that every woman liked to think she could have been Marilyn's friend. Fliss was convinced that, if nothing else, she understood the pressure of maintaining a public identity.

After collecting her case, she slid through the crowd like a ghost, went out into the bright sunshine, and found the taxi she'd booked waiting for her. Climbing into the back seat, she directed the driver to take her to Kerikeri. She felt a tangle of emotions: nervousness, excitement, sadness, despair, exhilaration, all rolled into one. She was so tired of the relentless rollercoaster. If she closed her eyes, she thought she might sleep for a week.

"Been here before?" the Maori driver asked cheerily.

"A long time ago." She looked out of the window. A lot would have changed since she'd last set eyes on the place. Her family had moved to Wellington when she was ten, after her father had died. It had been two weeks after the turn of the century—a new millennium, a new start. The first six months at her high school had been hard, but she'd soon adapted, finding living in the city much more exciting. Her sisters had been the same. Funny how back then she'd longed to travel, and now all she wanted was to come home.

"It's a great place, eh," the driver said, his voice carrying the distinctive Maori lilt. "Expanding all the time. A new Indian restaurant opened last week. Went there yesterday. Had an amazing Chicken Madras."

"Sounds great," she said, although she couldn't imagine she'd be eating out at all. Actually, she had no idea what she was going to do with herself over the next week or so with no work to take up her time. This wasn't a social visit, and she didn't have any hobbies.

She realized she hadn't turned on her phone after landing. It was still in her bag. Her fingers felt twitchy without the slim case in her hands, and her skin prickled at the thought of what she might be missing—what headlines, what news, what calls? Nobody knew where she was. Not her family, her friends, the press, not even her agent. And definitely not Jack. She felt as if she'd climbed on a boat and pushed off onto the ocean blue, heading for the horizon.

She could drown. The thought made her heart race. But it was also liberating. For the first time in her life, she was beholden to nobody.

Of course, she'd have to check in soon or they'd end up calling the police, thinking she'd been kidnapped or something. But she was going to have a few hours, at least, to herself, to get reacquainted with both the area and her oldest friend.

The taxi had taken the turning at the roundabout for Kerikeri, and they passed the occasional restaurant fronted by palm trees the shape of huge pineapples, and stalls on the side of the road selling bags of seasonal fruits—apples, feijoas, green kiwifruit, mandarins, and pears. There seemed to be more sky here, she thought, conscious of the lack of high-rise buildings. Even the city center only had one small, three-story office block standing out against the rest of the low shops and houses.

It felt warmer here, too. It was April, fall for the southern hemisphere. Well, autumn, she reminded herself. Her language had developed into an odd mix of American and Kiwi and sometimes she forgot which words to use where. In Wellington, the trees would be shedding their golden leaves, and the wind and rain meant that most people would have dug out their winter clothes already. Here, it had obviously been raining because the roads were wet, but now the sun was shining, and some people still wore shorts and tees. Most of the trees were evergreens, blending all four seasons into one.

She felt oddly disoriented, which was probably half jet lag, half her tumbling emotions. What time was it in LA? She forced her brain to calculate. It was Friday, about eleven a.m. here, so it must have been around four p.m. in LA. On Thursday—the day before. And now she had a headache.

"Where do you want me to drop you?" the taxi driver asked.

"The Post Office, please."

He turned right at the first roundabout and pulled up shortly afterward, next to the Post Office and opposite a small cinema. With shock, she saw that the poster out the front was advertising *Love for a Lifetime*, her latest movie. There she was, looking up lovingly at Jack, the leading actor, the guy who'd broken her heart, then taken the pieces and stomped all over them.

Suddenly, she felt naked, her whole life on show for all to point and laugh at. Her throat tightened so much, for a moment she couldn't breathe.

"Are you all right, love?" the driver asked with fatherly concern, watching her as she paid him. "You look a bit pale."

She swallowed hard. "I'm fine."

He frowned and leaned a little closer, peering at her face. "Do I know you? You look… familiar…"

"I'm nobody special." Feeling a wave of panic, she withdrew her credit card. "Thank you very much." She got out of the car before he could say anything else. After retrieving her case, she closed the door, and he pulled away.

She blew out a long, slow breath, and started walking along the path toward the high street.

Maybe this wasn't such a good idea after all. She'd thought of the Northland as a retreat, and had forgotten that, of course, they had cinemas and the internet. Perhaps she should have stayed at home, just turned off her phone, closed all the curtains, and done her best to ignore the reporters who continually thought up ingenious ways to invade her privacy.

Besides, it wasn't as if she was close to Roberta. They'd been best friends at primary school, but she hadn't seen her for eighteen years. They'd kept in touch sporadically via Facebook, email, and even the occasional phone call, but there was only so much you could say over the phone and on social media. Fliss had no idea whether Roberta would know what had been going on in her life over the past year. All she knew was that when she'd told Roberta she was having a difficult time and needed to get away, her friend had immediately said, "Come and stay with me."

She turned the corner and entered the high street. It was late morning, and the town was busy without being manic, filled with shoppers, the occasional tourist, and townsfolk going about their everyday business. She wandered past small clothing boutiques, shops selling souvenirs like fluffy toy kiwi birds and beautiful jewelry in the shape of Maori spiral korus and fish hooks, and cafés where customers were sitting outside, drinking lattes, and eating huge breakfasts that engulfed the plates and smelled wonderful as she walked past. Her stomach rumbled. She hadn't eaten a proper Kiwi full breakfast in years. She hadn't eaten a proper meal in years, period. She'd trained herself to think of food as a means to keep her body functioning, with coffee the only pleasure she hadn't been able to give up. Maybe she'd treat herself to something while she was here—some chocolate or ice cream. Go back to Wellington ten pounds heavier. That would give her mother something to snark about.

And then she saw it across the road—the Bay of Islands Brides shop, with Roberta's Bridal Café next to it.

Roberta had sent her photos of it, but it looked much bigger and prettier in real life. The signs above both shops bore wedding bells and flowers, and even from the other side of the road she could see that the dresses in the window were exquisite. The café was three-quarters full, the light jazz music spilling from the open door almost as tempting as the smell of freshly baked muffins.

Hefting her bag, she crossed the road, took a deep breath, and opened the door to the shop.

A bell jangled as she entered, and she let the door close behind her. Lifting her sunglasses onto the top of her head, she blinked at the sunlight that streamed in through the high windows. It was like coming to a shop for princesses. Racks filled with beautiful gowns of all shapes and sizes lined the left wall, while, on the right, shelves stacked with glittering tiaras, sparkling jewelry, and shoes of a hundred shades of white and cream made her feel weak at the knees.

There had been a time when she'd pictured herself in a place like this, buying her own wedding dress. Now, it was a fantasy she wasn't sure would ever come true.

"Good morning!" A slender woman in her fifties with silver hair cut in a neat bob and a ready smile approached her. "Can I help you?"

Fliss cleared her throat. "I was looking for Roberta."

The woman studied her for a moment with a slight frown. Her gaze slid down, taking in the white shirt, the designer jeans, the five-hundred-dollar sneakers, and the leather handbag, all of which Fliss was beginning to realize marked her as from the city.

Realization dawned on the woman's face. "Oh, of course, you must be Fliss. How lovely to meet you." She extended her hand. "I'm Roberta's mother; I'm Noelle."

Fliss vaguely remembered her from her childhood, this kind, gentle woman who'd always been so welcoming, who'd made the girls warm chocolate brownies with ice cream, and who'd never seemed cross or irritated with them. The fact that she used Fliss's nickname, and that her smile was genuine and her welcome unexpected after so many months of unpleasantness, made Fliss's eyes fill with tears.

"Oh no," Noelle said with alarm, "that wasn't supposed to happen!"

Fliss waved a hand. "I'm so sorry, it's not you, it's me, I'm just tired, and…"

"Of course, all that traveling, you must be exhausted," Noelle said. "Come in, come in. You can leave your case in my office, if you like, and then we'll get you a latte or something. That'll make you feel more human."

She led Fliss through the shop to the changing rooms at the back, all decorated in cream and painted with horseshoes and wedding bells, and through to an office. After locking Fliss's case in there, she then led her back through the shop.

"It's so beautiful in here." Despite her rising emotion, Fliss smiled at the sight of a young woman admiring herself in front of one of the mirrors while her mother titivated with her gown. "It must be a lovely place to work."

"It is." Noelle directed her past the shelves filled with accessories to the large archway in the wall that led through to the coffee shop. "Everyone's happy ninety-nine percent of the time. Of course, there's always some stress that goes with weddings, but we try to make sure everything is organized way in advance to eliminate some of that."

They entered the café, and Fliss followed Noelle over to the counter.

Immediately, she recognized Roberta, who was in the process of making coffee. She'd seen her in photos, but she would have recognized her anyway, because she'd hardly changed from the girl Fliss had once known, just several inches taller, and with slightly bigger boobs. The long-legged, dark-haired young woman glanced over at her, did a double take, and then a wonderful smile spread across her face.

"Fliss!" She came around the counter and threw her arms around Fliss's neck.

The two girls hugged, Fliss fighting back tears again at the welcome. "Hello, Bobcat," she said, using Roberta's childhood nickname.

"Jesus, I was hoping you'd forgotten that." Roberta laughed and squeezed her. "I'm so glad you came." She moved back and studied her friend, her eyes widening as she saw the emotion on Fliss's face. "Shit. What did I say?"

"She's tired," Noelle said smoothly, "and traveling can be exhausting. Why don't you make her a coffee? Libby will be here at midday, and then the two of you can shoot off and do some catching up."

Roberta glanced at her, obviously picking up her mother's attempt to cover Fliss's emotion, and she smiled. "Sure. What would you like? Cappuccino? Latte?"

"Trim latte, please."

"Do you want anything to eat? A muffin? The cheese and onion scones are delish, if I say so myself."

"No, thank you."

"Okay. Coffee coming right up."

"I'll leave you in Roberta's good hands," Noelle said. "But if you need anything at all while you're staying in Kerikeri, you just call me, okay?" She slid a card into Fliss's hand that bore the Bay of Islands Brides logo and her name and mobile number.

Still overcome by emotion, Fliss just nodded, and Noelle left to return to her customers.

Fliss slid the card into her pocket and sat at the empty table near the counter. Her eyes felt hot and scratchy. Noelle was right, she was tired, bone-tired. She couldn't remember a time when she hadn't been exhausted. Six months ago, her doctor had said it was depression and had prescribed medication for it. Looking across the shop, out of the window at the street, she wondered whether the pills had done her any good at all. They made her feel dull, and she certainly didn't feel as if she'd had any more energy since she'd started taking them. She wasn't sure she really had depression, not in the clinical sense of needing meds to replace missing chemicals. She was sad, that was all, and getting sadder by the day, and a doctor couldn't prescribe pills for that. Life was tough, and she'd thought that meds would help her cope with it, but the only drugs that would take away the pressures she found herself under weren't the kind she wanted to start getting involved with.

"Here you go." Roberta appeared and placed two cups on the table. She slid into the chair opposite and picked up her own coffee. Her green eyes studied Fliss over the rim of the cup. "So… long time no see! Do I ask how you are? Or shall we talk about something else?"

Chapter Two

"I wouldn't know where to start," Fliss said. "And I'm worried that I might start crying and not be able to stop."

"Probably better to wait until we're home, then," Roberta said cheerfully. "Tonight, we'll put on a chick flick and get out the red wine, and you can tell me everything then."

"Sounds great." Fliss felt a wave of relief that she didn't have to go through it straight away.

She glanced around the café, at the customers munching and sipping contentedly, most of them women who cooed as the girl in the wedding dress came into the doorway to show off her gown. "It looks as if you've been super successful here," she said. "I love the shop, and the bridal café is amazing." As well as muffins, the cabinet bore tiny cakes, all iced and decorated with a wedding theme, such as with miniature horseshoes, bells, and sprinklings of icing 'confetti'.

"That was my idea." Roberta sipped her coffee. "Phoebe and Bianca—you remember them, right? The twins. They're the ones with the flair for dressmaking, and Mum runs the shop. I could have just helped in the shop, but I wanted to do something myself, you know? So, I took a hospitality course and opened the café. I was terrified at first, but it's been brilliant."

"You do it all yourself?" Fliss asked. "You make all the cakes and everything?"

"Mostly." Roberta gestured at the younger woman currently serving at the counter. "Angie's full-time now she's left school, and she's great. And a friend, Libby—you'll meet her soon—she covers for me some afternoons, so I can have time off. She's got a marketing degree, so she's helpful for advertising and promotion, because that's something we don't know anything about. She's the one who came up with the idea of opening late on Thursdays, and we have fashion shows then.

We ask for volunteers to model some of the gowns and accessories, and I serve wine and canapés."

"It's just amazing." Fliss was full of admiration. "You've done so well for yourself."

"Well, I'm nowhere near your league." Roberta smiled.

Fliss looked at her cup and stirred her coffee. "You're probably happier though."

"Aw, jeez, are you trying to make me cry?" Roberta reached out and squeezed her hand.

Fliss gave her a bright smile. "So, what about your love life? Is there a man on the horizon?"

"Eh… I've been seeing a guy for a few months, but between you and me, I'm thinking of calling it quits."

"Oh, why?"

"Coby is nice enough, but he doesn't give me that zing, you know what I mean?"

"I do."

"He's convenient, and that's not really fair on him, because I think he wants more. He's good in bed, which is a point in his favor, but, well, that's not everything, is it?"

"No," Fliss said sadly. She glanced over as the young woman trying on dresses came out again in a different gown, her glowing face suggesting she thought she'd found the perfect dress. "Do you find it tough working here and being around all the wedding stuff? Do you feel any pressure to get married?"

Roberta watched the young woman twirl and laugh. "I don't know. Sometimes, I guess. I'm not really a girly girl like you, but I suppose we would all like to be a princess for a day."

Fliss smiled. Roberta had been a tomboy, and Fliss suspected her friend hadn't changed that much. She was currently wearing cropped jeans and a sleeveless white top. She'd pulled her long brown hair back in a simple ponytail, and wore very little makeup, very different from Fliss's own carefully applied foundation, concealer, powder, eyeliner, lip liner, and lipstick, all made to look as if she wasn't wearing any at all. How nice to just get up in the morning, slick on some lip gloss, tie up your hair, and walk out of the door. Fliss took a good hour straightening her hair and putting on her makeup. She had to, because she couldn't afford to be plastered across the internet with shadows under her eyes or wild hair.

"You've not changed," Roberta said. "You were always very girly. You were the one who liked high heels and handbags and sequins."

"I suppose we're quite different, really," Fliss said. "And yet, you were the only friend who offered me a place to stay."

Roberta's brow furrowed. "I suppose all your friends are famous too?"

"I don't have a lot of friends." It was difficult to admit. "I have a lot of acquaintances. But it's hard to know whom to trust in the business. Lots of people are only out for themselves. When your star is rising, it's amazing how many people want to be your friend. But when something like this happens, you look around for support and suddenly realize you're completely alone."

Pity filled Roberta's eyes. "That's fucking horrible," she said fiercely.

"I'm sorry." Fliss cursed herself. "I sound terribly self-pitying and pathetic. I don't mean to be."

"Don't apologize," Roberta said, her voice firm. "I don't want to hear the words 'I'm sorry' again while you're here. You've done nothing wrong, and you have every reason to hate the world right now. While you're here, you can swear and cry and yell and moan all you like. You don't have to put on an act with me."

Fliss's bottom lip trembled, and she bit it hard. "You don't know what that means to me."

Roberta waved a hand. She leaned back in her chair, and her eyes gleamed. "How's your mum?"

Fliss sniffed and gave her a wry look, and Roberta laughed. "No change, huh?"

"Twice as bad, if you must know."

"She was pretty bad back then. I'll always remember coming into your house eating a burger. She marched me to the mirror and pointed out the spot on my chin and the puppy fat around my waist, and then made me throw the burger in the bin. I was ten. Talk about ruin your self-esteem and give you a complex."

"Welcome to my world. She's the main reason I haven't eaten a real meal for, like, twenty years." Fliss glanced at Noelle, who was talking to a customer in the shop. "You're so lucky with your mum. She was always really nice to me, and she doesn't seem to have changed."

"She hasn't. I am lucky, I know that."

"I was so sorry to hear about your dad." Roberta had emailed her when her father had died over a year ago.

Roberta sighed. "Yeah, that was tough on all of us. On the surface of it, Mum coped well, although you never know how people are dealing with it deep down, do you? But I suppose she had to be strong for the rest of us."

"I guess you all took it hard."

"Phoebe especially, because she was the one who found him. She's had a real tough time."

"At least she has Rafe now," Fliss said. Roberta had told her how Phoebe had struggled with her father's death, falling into depression for months after. She'd then become obsessed with running, had entered marathons, and trained for a triathlon, and she'd been planning to move to Auckland to work in a bigger bridal shop. Unfortunately, she'd been in an accident, had been knocked on the head, and lost her memory for a while. But she'd gone on to marry her boyfriend and stay in Kerikeri, and Roberta had said the two of them seemed to be happy.

"What about Bianca and your brothers?" she wanted to know.

"Bianca's okay. Better now Phoebe has decided to stay. Elliot's Elliot, a pain in the arse, no change there. He's a cop. You'd never know it when he's not in uniform—he's as mischievous as ever."

"What about Dominic?" Fliss could just remember Roberta's oldest brother. He'd been four years older and had seemed moody and mysterious to the young Fliss. He'd been great at sport, and Fliss had gone with his family to watch him play soccer, rugby, and cricket at the high school. She remembered going home one evening and dreaming about him in his cricket whites, fantasizing that he might ask her out. He never did, of course, and she'd moved away not long after. Would he still remember her?

"Yeah, he's had a bit of a tough time," Roberta said. "He met a girl, Jo, and married young, and they had a daughter, Emily. She's seven now. You'll meet her later, because he drops her off at my house on the days I'm home, after he's picked her up from school. Then, about… uh… two years ago now, I suppose, Jo died."

"Oh, no."

"Yeah, right out of the blue. She had an asthma attack while they were at the beach, didn't have her inhaler on her, and was dead by the time the ambulance got to the hospital. Such a shock. And then, of course, Dad died a year later. So, Dom's been through the mill a bit.

He's all right though, he's one of the good guys." She looked up, past Fliss, and smiled. "Here's Libby. Guess it's home time!"

Fliss turned to see a blonde of around her own age approaching. Her face looked familiar, and suddenly she recognized her. Libby had been two years above her and Roberta at school, in Elliot's year. Fliss remembered her as being very plump, with pigtails, and terrible sticky-out teeth. Libby was now sexy and shapely, her hair pinned up in a messy bun, and when she smiled, she had beautiful straight teeth.

"Fliss!" Libby came over to her and kissed her on the cheek. "How lovely to see you."

"And you." Fliss returned the kiss and stepped back. "Wow, you look amazing."

"Ha! No more Bugs Bunny for me," Libby said with a grin. "And yeah, I've lost a bit of weight, although it's a struggle to keep it off, especially working here." She pulled a face at the sight of Angie walking past her with a tray of cakes for some of the customers.

Roberta laughed. "Okay, we're off, then. You all good for the day?"

"Yep. You two go and enjoy yourselves." Libby picked up an apron from behind the counter, slipped it over her head, and fastened it around her waist. "Maybe we'll catch up one evening or something?" she said to Fliss as she began to prepare a coffee order.

"Sounds lovely," Fliss said sincerely, feeling wistful that her stay was only temporary. How she would love to have a circle of friends like this.

Then she scolded herself as she got up and watched Roberta go off to get her case from Noelle's office. No doubt they all envied her fame and fortune. It was so easy to think the grass was greener on the other side. Her life hadn't all been doom and gloom; she'd had some amazing times, and in fact it was only recently that everything had turned to custard, to coin a New Zealand phrase.

And yet, she couldn't deny a deep envy of these women and their carefree lives. She watched Libby munch on a chocolate muffin as she worked, clearly not thinking about the calorie content or the fact that it wasn't low carb. And then Roberta appeared, laughing at something Noelle had said, the thought never entering her head that someone in the shop might be watching her, maybe even filming her, intent on spitefully ruining her life because they were jealous that they didn't have what she had. A woman by the door had glanced at Fliss and done a double-take; now she and her friend were staring, obviously sure they recognized her.

Roberta came over, her brow furrowing as she took in Fliss's expression. "Are you okay?"

Fliss nodded. "Let's go."

They waved to the others and headed toward the door. As they passed the two women sitting by the window, one reached out and grabbed Fliss's arm. "Hey, you're Felicity Rivers!" The woman's jaw dropped, her eyes lighting with excitement. "I saw you in *Love for a Lifetime* last night!"

"She wishes," Roberta said, pulling Fliss away from the woman's hand and moving in front of her as if she were her bodyguard. "She's always getting mistaken for her, aren't you, Jane?"

Fliss nodded, panic making her heart race. "I wouldn't be an actress if you paid me," she said, adding a light laugh and rolling her eyes.

The woman's smile faded. "Oh. I was so sure you were her! I like her. The movie was amazing. So much chemistry between her and Jack Leeson—it was obvious he was crazy about her. So sad what's happened between the two of them, don't you think?"

"Absolutely," Roberta said, opening the door and steering Fliss out. She let the door swing shut behind her and gestured for Fliss to follow her. "Jesus. I'm so sorry about that."

"Don't worry about it. It's not the first time something like that has happened, and it won't be the last. I'm just glad she liked the movie." Her lips twisted. Obviously, the woman had been wrong, because even though Fliss had fallen heavily for him, Jack had proven that whatever he was feeling for her, it wasn't love.

"Oh Christ. I think it's going to be a two-bottles-of-wine night tonight." Roberta slid her arm through Fliss's. "Come on. Let's go home and then you can relax properly, without worrying about having the eyes of the world on you."

Fliss looked out of the window as Roberta drove out of town. The sky had darkened with thick gray clouds, and sure enough, as they headed for the small settlement of Waimate North, large drops of rain began to pepper the windscreen. She'd forgotten how quickly the weather could change in the Northland, truly four seasons in one day. Still, it didn't detract from the beauty of the landscape. The orchards and buildings gave way to open fields and rolling countryside, the hills dotted with cows and sheep.

"You don't live in town, then?" Fliss said, surprised. She'd expected Roberta to be in the middle of Kerikeri.

"I did. I shared a house with Libby. But then she moved in with Mike, her boyfriend, and… I don't know, I needed a change. I've always wanted to have my own garden and grow vegetables."

"Seriously?" Fliss laughed. "You don't strike me as the vegetable growing type."

"I have a great veggie garden. I'm expecting you to help me dig it." Roberta cast an eye up as the rain began to hammer on the car and pool on the road. "Maybe not until the sun comes out, though."

Fliss smiled, thinking how strange it was going to be, staying in a true country house. She'd lived in cities for so long, she'd forgotten that not everyone enjoyed high-rise buildings and public transport and easy access to the gyms and salons.

Her eyes widened when Roberta eventually slowed the car and turned onto a drive that swept in front of a long, low, stone-built house. It was so far removed from her exquisite apartment in LA that it was almost funny. Surrounded by apple and orange trees, the house looked old but well-maintained and had possibly been a farmhouse in the past.

"Do you own the fields on either side?" Fliss asked as Roberta parked and they got out.

"Yes, although you needn't look so impressed—the soil's not good for much, which was why the place was so cheap. I let my neighbor use them for his cows to keep the grass down. I like the idea that nobody can build right next to me." She opened the front door. "Come in."

Fliss entered and found herself in a low-ceilinged living room, with a large hearth on the far wall. The sofa and chairs were covered with colorful throws, and the floor with a variety of mismatched rugs. A gray cat rose and padded over to greet them, while another, smaller gray cat jumped off the sofa and fled along the corridor.

"Jasmine's friendly," Roberta said, bending to stroke her, "but Rosie doesn't like strangers. She'll warm to you after a while."

"Didn't picture you as a crazy cat lady," Fliss teased, stroking Jasmine as she rubbed up against her legs.

"Oh, I'm totally going to be found covered in hair and half-eaten by Alsatians." Roberta went over to the sliding glass doors and opened them, and Fliss followed her out into the back garden.

A large wooden deck ran the length of the house, covered by a slanting roof to keep off the rain. Comfortable-looking outdoor chairs with cushions and a low table filled with magazines and an empty wine bottle or two suggested Roberta spent a lot of her time here.

There were chickens to the left, several vegetable patches to the right, and a neatly tended lawn in the middle circled by borders filled with a myriad of untidy flowers.

"It's gorgeous," Fliss said, surprising herself with a surge of envy.

"I'm in heaven." Roberta put her hands on her hips. "Jeez, look at that." A piece of corrugated plastic had slid off the top of the hen house. "I'll have to put that back on when it stops raining."

"I'll help."

"Not in those shoes, you won't."

"I'll get changed," Fliss said, picking up her case. She was glad she'd brought some comfortable clothes with her. This was no place for designer jeans and expensive shoes!

"I'll show you your room." Roberta led her back indoors. They passed a kitchen that had herbs hanging from the ceiling, jars full of homemade pickles and jams, and shelves of various spices. A crockpot sat on the table, and Roberta checked it quickly, filling the room with the smell of chicken casserole as she gave it a quick stir. "Dinner," she said, continuing down a long corridor. "There's the bathroom." She gestured to an open door. "And here's your room."

Fliss went in. It was smallish compared to what she was used to, but the bed was a king, covered with a handmade quilt and huge white pillows. The room smelled of lavender and rosemary. The windows overlooked the veggie patches, and the walls bore large paintings of a cat that looked just like Jasmine.

"Did you paint these?" Fliss asked.

"I did. They're not great, but I like doing them."

Fliss swallowed hard. While she'd been going from party to party, trying to impress agents, just trying to be seen, Roberta had been slowly making herself a home and pouring her soul into her creative projects.

Her eyes filled with tears. "I love it," she said, her voice little more than a squeak. "Thank you so much."

"Aw, come here." Roberta enveloped her in a hug. "I'm absolutely thrilled you're here. I'll go and put the kettle on, and you take your time to unpack. We'll have some lunch, and then maybe later we'll tackle the hen house." She gave Fliss a final squeeze, then left the room.

Fliss sat on the edge of the bed, looking out at the garden. The rain was already lessening, leaving the garden glowing like a jewel as the sun came out. The leaves and grass shone, and everything seemed fresh and bright and full of hope.

So why did she feel so low? Maybe because she wasn't here to stay, and therefore any hope she felt was as insubstantial as a bubble, ready to pop at any moment. She was stupid if she thought she could escape her real life. Having her phone turned off was almost making her feel sick. The notion of how angry her agent was going to be only added to her nausea. And as for when she thought of Jack, who must be filled with smug glee at her current situation... No amount of feeding chickens or digging vegetable gardens was going to solve her problems.

But sinking into self-pity wouldn't get her anywhere. She was here now, and she might as well make the most of it.

Wiping her face and taking a deep breath, she opened her case and began to search for something more suitable to wear.

Chapter Three

"I think I'm pregnant," the sixteen-year-old girl said.

Dominic let out a long breath. The pastoral notes on the computer screen told him that Lara had been sent out of class three times that week for misbehaving, but each time in her interview with the Dean on duty, she'd refused to talk. Eventually, one of the Deans had flagged her on Dominic's list, hoping he might have more luck in deciphering her escalating behavior. She'd come to his office reluctantly, had sat there with her arms crossed, mute and angry, and after about ten minutes of asking questions without receiving any answers, he'd assumed she wasn't going to talk to him either. And then, suddenly, she'd come out with that revelation.

She bit her lip hard and lifted her chin, but a tear trickled down her cheek.

He passed her the box of tissues from his desk and leaned forward, his elbows on his knees. "All right," he said softly, "it's not the end of the world." He stifled a sigh. It was a partial truth. An unplanned pregnancy at such a young age didn't carry quite the social stigma it had in the past, but there was no doubt that her life would change significantly if she were to have a baby, and not necessarily for the better.

As a school counselor, Dominic was available most of the time in his office if students needed to talk to someone, whether it was about school matters concerning exams or a teacher, issues with other students, or personal problems with friends or family. Sometimes, weeks went by where the most serious case he had was a student panicking because they hadn't done their homework. This week, he'd dealt with two teens who'd been charged with shoplifting, a boy who was clearly being beaten by his father, three students who'd been caught smoking marijuana, two bullying incidents, and a girl who Dominic suspected had been sexually abused by an uncle. And now

Lara claiming she was pregnant. Was there something in the water? Or was it a full moon?

He glanced again at the computer screen he always angled carefully away from the student's chair. Lara's mother had passed away when she was seven. Her father had remarried when she was nine to a woman who'd brought with her two children by her first marriage. Lara and her stepmother didn't get on, and she'd run away from home several times. She'd been in and out of trouble ever since she'd come up to the high school.

He looked back at her, pity outweighing his initial frustration at her rebellious attitude. A settled family life didn't guarantee a student's success, but there was no doubt that a lack of parental guidance was a recurring factor in the majority of troubled students who passed through his office.

"Don't yell at me," Lara said.

"I won't," he replied. "It's not my place to judge you. I'm on your side, and I'm here to help."

Her bottom lip trembled. Maybe, he thought, it was the first time in her life she'd ever been told that.

"I should start," he told her, "by saying that if you'd rather see a female counselor instead of me, that's okay, and I can see if one is free right now."

She shook her head. "I want to talk to you."

"Okay. That's fine."

She swallowed hard. "My Dad's going to kill me," she whispered. "My friend Sasha said I should say that Matt raped me, then it wouldn't be my fault and Dad wouldn't be so angry with me."

Dominic held her gaze. "Did he rape you, Lara?"

She licked her lips. Then, eventually, she lowered her eyes. "Sasha said it was rape because I wasn't sure, and he talked me into it." She swallowed and said in a small voice, "Do you think that makes it rape?"

He didn't say anything for a moment, conscious of the fine line he had to walk. This very issue had been discussed at the latest meeting of Northland school counselors, with everyone very aware that although it was great that girls were encouraged nowadays to speak up against sexual abuse, it did leave young men open to spurious accusations of rape. The meeting had become very heated at points, as everyone had their own views on where the line in the sand should be drawn. Dominic had done his best to remain pragmatic rather than get drawn into discussions about the changing roles of men and women in society, and he decided to do the same today.

"If you said no loudly at any point," he told Lara, "or made it clear in other ways that you didn't want to have sex, and he ignored you and continued anyway, then that's rape, and the young man deserves to be reported. But if you consented to having sex, and then afterward you wished you hadn't… It's very difficult. Only you know how much he pushed you, and how clear you made your consent. The decision must be yours, and if you tell me now with your hand on your heart that you did not want to have sex with this young man and he coerced you into it, I will back you all the way. But if you only want to accuse him so that you don't have to accept responsibility for your actions, or because you want to punish him, you should think very carefully. A rape accusation is serious, and could destroy the young man's life, which would be a travesty if it were to be false."

Tears rolled down her face. "He didn't rape me," she whispered. "I was nervous, but I never said no. I liked him. And I wanted to know what it was like."

Dominic nodded, relieved. "Good girl. I'm proud of you for admitting that. So, let's talk about what happens now, okay? Have you taken a pregnancy test?"

"No."

"Is your period late?"

Lara blinked. "Um… no."

"So, what makes you think you might be pregnant?"

"Because Sasha said so. I mean, we only did it once, and he said I couldn't get pregnant the first time, but Sasha says you can."

He stifled a sigh. In some schools, the guidance counselors held the sex education classes. Dominic was happy to leave that to the Health and Physical Education teachers at his school, but it wouldn't be the first time that he'd had to put a student right about sex.

"In this case, Sasha is right, you can get pregnant the first time you have sex, although it doesn't mean that you are, necessarily. You didn't use a condom?"

"No. We should have, I know."

"It's best if you do because then you don't have to worry about pregnancy or disease, but let's focus on what you do from now on."

"He didn't come inside me," she said. Her face turned scarlet, but to her credit she didn't look away. "He... um... pulled out and... you know... in his hand. Does that make a difference?"

Thinking how much he and his brother would have laughed if they'd been told as youngsters that he'd be giving sex advice to teenagers for a living, Dominic said, "Okay, well, again, you can still get pregnant because there are sperm in the fluid that leaks out before a man ejaculates. But it makes it more unlikely. Look, the best thing is if I send you over to the nurse, because she has some pregnancy kits there. Why don't you take the test, and, once you know, you can come back and talk about what happens next."

Lara nodded, so he picked up the phone and dialed the nurse. "Mrs. Phillips? Do you have five minutes for Lara Taylor, please?"

"Is she pregnant?" Nora Phillips asked him.

"Probably not," he said. "Needs a bit of clarification."

"Virgin birth?" They'd had another girl a few months ago who was terrified she'd gotten pregnant after having oral sex with a young man.

He stifled a laugh. "Not quite. But best to be sure."

"Send her over."

He hung up and sent Lara on her way.

Then he leaned back in his chair and blew out a breath. That had been a tricky one. Luckily, it was Friday, and the bell was due to go soon. He wasn't sure he could handle anything else today.

The counselors' secretary, Vivien, poked her head around the door, then came in with a cup of tea.

"Thank you," he said gratefully.

"Thought you might need it," Vivien said. "Lara Taylor's a few sandwiches short of a picnic."

He smiled but didn't answer. Lara wasn't dumb, just misinformed. It wasn't her fault that she'd gotten her only information about sex from other clueless teenagers.

Vivien hesitated, a flush appearing on her cheeks.

"Thank you for the tea," he said gently, turning his gaze back to his computer.

She hovered for another few seconds, then turned and left.

Pursing his lips, he opened the blinds and turned his chair to look out over the large circle of lawn they called The Green as he sipped his tea. At some point, he was going to have to talk to Vivien and tell her directly that he wasn't interested in a relationship. She'd been dropping hints ever since she started at the school six months before, not that he'd ever given her any sign that he was looking for love. Quite the opposite. On the day he'd buried his wife, Dominic had sworn to himself that he'd never look at another woman again, and so far, he'd kept it.

He didn't regret that vow at all. He'd loved his wife with every cell in his body, and he always would. No other woman could ever come close to replacing her.

But sticking to his word had a high price. He leaned his head on the back of the chair and finally admitted the truth. He was lonely. At thirty-two, he had a lot of years ahead of him, years that he should have spent with his wife by his side. He missed her, physically, emotionally, mentally—every way a man could miss a woman. His mind longed for the intimate conversation and comfort that a close relationship brought, and his body ached for someone warm and soft to share his bed. But it was pointless to dwell on it because it only made him agitated, so he pushed it to the back of his mind.

He felt a sweep of sorrow for Lara. Her mother had died when Lara was seven—the same age Dominic's daughter was now. In fact, she would be eight in a few months' time. He knew that although puberty could start in girls as young as eight, it was more likely to be from around the age of ten, but it would be good to make sure Emily was well informed, as he'd hate her to be as ignorant as Lara about her own body, and sex.

A year or so ago, Emily had asked where babies come from, and he'd sat with her and given her a basic talk, a similar one, he was sure, that Nora Phillips was giving Lara right at that moment. But he hadn't yet explained the details about menstruation, or other ways her body might change. He'd been waiting for her to ask, because girls always seemed to know more than boys; they talked amongst themselves, and he was sure that at least one of her friends would have an older sister, which would prompt a discussion amongst the girls about bras and tampons and send them home asking for more information from their parents.

But what if she didn't ask? Briefly, he toyed with the notion of getting one of his sisters to talk to Emily—maybe Roberta, as his daughter spent a lot of time at her house after school while he did his rounds in the community. But that wasn't fair. It was his responsibility.

He felt a twist inside at the thought that it should be Jo giving her the talk, buying Emily her first sanitary products, taking her to have her first bra fitted. Girls need their mothers, just as boys need their fathers. Working at the high school, he'd seen many single parents cope marvelously because they had to, but that didn't mean kids didn't need both a mother and father around. He believed in the strength of the family unit, and it broke his heart to think that Emily was growing up without her mother's guidance. It was hard enough being a dad; how was he supposed to fill Jo's shoes too?

His phone rang, and he answered it, "Dominic Goldsmith."

"She's not pregnant," Nora said. "Thought you'd want to know."

He blew out a relieved breath. "Good."

"I'll have a chat with her about a few things, try to put her right."

"Thanks, Nora."

"She might come and see you Monday, though. She said you were the first person she'd ever spoken to who was on her side."

He flicked his pen on and doodled in the margin of his notebook. "I do my best."

"You're one of the good guys, Dominic. Have a great weekend."

"You too." He hung up.

You're one of the good guys. He hoped so. Being a school counselor wasn't the easiest job in the world. Many parents objected to the fact that a student's conversation with him was confidential, and that he was under no obligation to tell the parents anything, including whether the student requested information about contraception or an abortion. Personally, he knew he'd be angry if, when Emily was sixteen, he was to discover that someone at the school had arranged for her to be on the pill without him knowing. But from the student's point of view, it was important that they felt he wasn't going to go running back to their parents if they discussed something with him.

Over the road, the primary school bell rang, and he sighed and started tidying away his things, knowing it wouldn't be long before Emily appeared. Sure enough, by the time the high school bell went five minutes later, Emily was at the door, and she came in and threw her arms around his neck.

He hugged her back, squeezing her tightly, knowing it wouldn't be long before she felt too self-conscious to show him affection in public. She wasn't quite as worldly-wise as some of her friends yet, but every day she seemed a little more grown up.

"You're squishing me," she said, and he let her go. She still wore her long brown hair in braids, but he was sure she'd ask to have it cut soon in a more modern style. How he wished he could wrap her in cotton wool and keep her at home, so she'd never grow up. But that wasn't an option, unfortunately.

"Did you have a good day?" he asked her.

She perched on the edge of his desk. "Miss Lawrence said my somersaults were so amazing that I should join the gymnastics club."

"Would you like that?" he asked. He'd been good at several sports in his youth, and he liked the thought that she might be following in his footsteps.

"Yes, Kaia said she'd go with me. She can't keep her legs straight when she does a cartwheel, but she can stand on her hands for ages."

"Then you should both go. What night is it?"

"Mondays."

"I can drop you off there after school and pick you up when you've finished."

"Okay, Dad. Are we going to Roberta's now?"

"Yep." The bell rang, and he stood, shouldered his laptop case, and collected an armful of folders to work on later that evening. "Come on."

Chapter Four

Dominic and his daughter walked through the school to the car. It was raining hard, and they ducked between the various shade sails over the paths, trying to avoid the throng of students desperate to get off the school grounds in the first five minutes. Once in the car, they navigated the busy roads until they were out of town, and then Dominic put his foot down and headed out into the countryside as the rain eased off and the sun came out.

"Dad," Emily said.

"Hmm?"

"Do you think you'll get married again?"

The comment was so unexpected that he stared at his daughter, startled. "What made you say that?"

"Just wondered."

"No, honey. I'm not getting married again. Your mum was the only woman for me," he reassured her, not wanting her to worry that someone was going to come in and take her mother's place.

"I think you should," she said.

Now he was really bemused. "What?"

"I was talking to Kaia. She's going to be a bridesmaid when her mum marries Wiremu in May. I'd *looooove* to do that again." Emily had been a bridesmaid at her aunt Phoebe's wedding back in February. She'd loved her dress so much that for a whole week she'd put it on as soon as she came home from school and had refused to take it off until she went to bed.

"I'm sure Elliot or Roberta or Bianca will get married eventually," he said. "You can probably be a bridesmaid then."

"Don't you want to get married again, though?" She sounded disappointed.

"No," he said, frowning. "Just because your mum isn't here doesn't mean I don't love her anymore." He waved his left hand at her, showing her his wedding ring.

"Kaia said the marriage vows say, 'till death do us part'."

"Yes…" he said slowly.

"So… Mum's gone. Why are you still wearing it?"

He returned his hand to the steering wheel. His daughter's attitude had completely taken him by surprise, and he felt oddly hurt by it. "Because I'm still married to her in my heart, and I don't want that to change." His voice came out sharper than he'd meant.

Emily swallowed. "I didn't mean to upset you, Daddy."

He reached out and took her hand. "It's okay. I know it's been a few years now, and you were so young when she died."

"I… I'm having trouble remembering her," she whispered, her bottom lip trembling. "I'm sorry."

That made his eyes sting, but he smiled at her. "Don't be sorry. It's not your fault."

"I still love her, Dad."

"I know, sweetie." He slowed down as he approached the drive to Roberta's house. "Come on, chin up. I bet Jasmine can't wait to play with you today."

"I brought that new toy we found," she said, producing a mouse with a bell on the end that they'd discovered in the hospice charity shop.

He parked in front of the house and turned off the engine. "Go on then, see if she likes it."

Emily got out and ran into the house. Dominic checked the clock on the dash. He was supposed to be back in town in twenty minutes. He ran through the list of people he wanted to visit, then tossed the list onto the passenger seat as he changed his outfit for his afternoon job.

When he'd done, he sat there for a minute, summoning the energy to move. Emily's offhand comment about removing his wedding ring had upset him. He held it up, feeling old and outdated. All around him, he could see the family unit breaking up. Fewer and fewer people were getting married. And even if they were, a good half went on to get divorced. Kids often had multiple siblings by different fathers. Loyalty and love weren't in vogue now. It was all about the pleasures of the flesh, and nobody cared about the beauty of the soul.

Then his lips twisted. Elliot would have laughed aloud at that thought and said *What are you, thirty-two or eighty-two?* His brother was respectful of his beliefs, but he did tease him about his archaic attitude sometimes.

But what was wrong with having higher expectations of people? Of wanting more than a blaze of lust followed by a life of discontent?

Okay, he could see how a brief blaze of lust wouldn't be the worst thing in the world. But even though his sex-starved body craved companionship, his soul hungered for something more.

Impatient with his wistful mood, he got out of the car and went into the house. Emily was alone in the living room, playing with Jasmine. "They're outside," she said.

"They?"

"Roberta and her friend. I don't know her name. Roberta said to wait here because it's muddy and they'd be in soon."

Remembering her saying something about an old friend coming to stay from America, he went through the sliding doors and into the garden.

There, he found Roberta and a slender blonde woman struggling to put a sheet of corrugated plastic back on the top of the hen house. The recent shower had turned the earth to mud, and the two of them were slipping about as they tried to lift the plastic.

"Can I help?" he asked as he approached.

The two women turned, startled at his voice. The plastic slipped out of Roberta's hand, and the sheet spun and hit the blonde in the shoulder. She stepped back, caught her gumboots on a low rock, slipped, and landed on her backside in the mud. It sprayed up, covering her completely in big, gooey droplets.

Roberta stared at her, then burst out laughing. She looked over at her brother and grinned. "Talk about an untimely interruption."

"I'm so sorry." Mortified, he came forward and held out a hand. "I distracted you both—I do apologize."

The young woman looked at his hand for a moment, then placed hers into it. He pulled her up, a little too quickly, and she bumped against him.

"Sorry," he said, not really meaning it. Even though she was agitated, embarrassed, and covered in mud, he could see she was gorgeous. Her blonde hair was twisted up with a clip, leavings strands to fall around her pale face. She was possibly the most classically beautiful woman he'd ever seen, with a pair of amazing turquoise eyes that were now staring up at him in complete shock.

"Dominic?" she said. She brushed back a lock of hair, unwittingly smearing a blob of mud across her cheek.

He frowned. "Do I know you?" Surely, he would have remembered if he'd met her before.

"This is Fliss Rivers," Roberta said, sounding amused. "I went to primary school with her, but she left in year six."

Dominic had a vague recollection of the skinny girl who'd been glued to his sister's side. The two of them had sometimes come to the high school to watch him play sport. He seemed to remember a certain cricket match where he'd grabbed a bottle of water from them in between overs. It had been a roasting hot day, and he'd stripped off his cricket jumper and replaced it with a white tee from his bag. He'd turned around to discover that they'd been watching him; the blonde girl had blushed scarlet, and Roberta had dissolved into a fit of giggles. He'd walked off, half exasperated, and half amused.

"I remember you," he said. "You've grown up a lot since then."

She blinked as if uncertain how to take that, her gaze sliding down him. Her eyes widened, and her jaw dropped. "Holy shit," she said, "you're wearing a dog collar."

He'd forgotten he'd put it on and touched his hand to it. "Well, we call it a clerical collar, and we don't tend to call shit holy, but you're on the right track."

Her face went as red as it had all those years ago on the cricket pitch. "And now I've said holy shit in front of a priest. I'm so sorry."

He laughed. "I'm not a priest, I'm a deacon, and Roberta can vouch for the fact that I still swear, so don't worry about it."

"He does," Roberta said. "More fucks than a Victorian brothel."

Fliss's lips curved up and her color died down a little, although her cheeks retained their rosy hue. "Well, it's nice to meet you again," she said. "But I'd better go and get changed."

"Nice to meet you too," he said. "I've got to go in a minute, but I'll be back later to pick up Emily."

Fliss nodded. "See you later." She lowered her eyes and slipped past him into the house.

Dominic met Roberta's amused gaze and gave her a wry look. "Don't say a word."

"Wouldn't dream of it." She gestured at the corrugated sheet. "Give us a hand?"

He helped her lift the plastic on top of the hen house and held it while she nailed it down. As she banged in the last nail, she glanced across at him with a grin. "You're itching to ask."

"No, I'm not."

"Liar."

"You'd say that to a man of God?"

She laughed and started packing up her tools. "So... don't tell me you don't recognize her."

"I do," he said. "Just. Something about a cricket match and her blushing while you giggled."

"I'd forgotten about that. But that's not what I meant. Seriously, you don't recognize her?"

He frowned. "I don't know what you mean."

"She's Felicity Rivers." She waited for his reaction. He pursed his lips, and she frowned. "Honestly, you're so dense. She's an actress. She's in *Love for a Lifetime*, that new movie? She's on the poster outside the cinema."

"Oh." Had he heard of the movie? Possibly.

"Whitfield wants her for his new thriller," Roberta said.

He had heard of Max Whitfield, the famous director whose movies were guaranteed to be box office hits. "I didn't realize." He wasn't sure what to make of that information. He'd never met anyone famous. Was he supposed to be impressed?

He followed Roberta back into the house. She put the tools in a cupboard, then returned to the living room and scooped Emily up into her arms. "Hey, Monkey!"

"Hey, Bobcat!"

Roberta kissed the girl's neck, and she squealed.

Dominic gestured along the corridor to where Fliss had disappeared into the bathroom. "So, what's she doing here?"

Roberta hesitated and glanced at Emily, who'd sat back down with the cat. "Just taking a break," she said. She gestured for him to follow her out.

He bent and kissed Emily on the top of her head. "See you in a bit, sweetheart."

"Bye, Daddy."

Leaving her playing with Jasmine, he followed Roberta out to his car.

"Didn't want to say in front of her," his sister said softly. "It's best if we don't tell her in case she tells anyone at school. The press would pay good money to find Fliss at the moment."

"Why?"

"She's had a really tough time over the past six months or so."

"Oh?" Dominic wasn't into gossip, but he was interested to know why this apparently famous actress had come to the back-end of a country at the bottom of the world, to a house in the middle of nowhere, where there would be no grand parties, no contacts to make, and no designer clothes. "If Whitfield is after her, she must be doing fairly well for herself."

"Oh, on the surface of it she's on the verge of stardom. She had a few minor TV roles, then a couple of smaller movies, and then landed the lead part in *Love for a Lifetime*," she said. "And because of that, she's been offered the role in Whitfield's new thriller. It's her big break. She'll be an A-list actress after this."

"So, what's the problem?"

"Well, she fell heavily for the lead actor in *Love for a Lifetime*—Jack Leeson. It was all over the internet. They were the golden couple while they were filming. Then they broke up. He's said publicly that she told him he'd hold her back and she has her sights set on the lead actor in Whitfield's movie, but I'm not going to believe anything I read online. Anyway, Leeson was furious, as much by her getting the role as being dumped, I'm sure. So, he released a photo of her that he had on his phone."

"I'm guessing it's not a photo of her having tea with his mother."

"Not quite, no. It's not that lewd; she's in a bathrobe. It's very sexy though. I'm surprised you haven't seen it. It's all over the Internet. But the thing is, he's threatening to sell a whole bunch more, including a video of her. He's getting offers from everywhere, hundreds of thousands of dollars. Selling his soul for his five minutes of fame." Roberta's voice was full of disgust.

"Poor girl." Dominic's heart went out to the beautiful, gentle creature he'd just picked out of the mud.

"She's horrified and humiliated. Apparently, the movie company is talking about dropping her, which is disgusting because they're getting more publicity than ever at the moment because of it. The thing is, she's not young, she's twenty-eight, which is old for Hollywood. If this goes pear-shaped, that's her done. It's doubtful she'd ever get a chance like this again."

"So, she's come here to escape?"

Roberta nodded. "She needed to get away, and what better place than the Northland? The press doesn't know she's here yet, and hopefully we can keep it that way."

"I won't tell anyone," he said.

His sister smiled at that and reached up to kiss his cheek. "I know you won't, sweetie."

"I'd better be off."

"I've got a chicken casserole on, if you want to stay for dinner when you're done."

He hesitated. "Probably best not to. I'm sure it's the last thing she'd want."

Roberta's lips curved up. "Oh, I don't know. She still looks at you the way she did on the cricket pitch that day."

He laughed. "Yeah, right. I'll catch you later." He got into the car, waved goodbye, and headed for the road.

As he drove, though, he remembered the way Fliss had stared at him, the look in her eyes as she'd said his name. It made him smile, and he accepted the compliment, then dismissed it. He had more important things to think about than some actress who'd soon return to her life of glitz and glamor.

Still, his vocation was to serve, to help those in need, and if anyone was in need right now, it appeared to be Fliss Rivers.

Chapter Five

Fliss stood under the shower, letting the hot water cascade over her. God only knew what Dominic thought of her, falling on her butt in that puddle in such an ungainly fashion, splashing mud across her clothes and face like a child. Not that it mattered what he thought.

And yet, she wanted him to like her. When he'd pulled her up and she'd bumped against him, he'd looked down at her and her heart had skipped a beat. He had short brown hair that was going gray at the temples, and his bright green eyes had held more than a hint of warmth. Although maybe he'd just recognized Felicity Rivers and had been impressed at having a famous person in his sister's house. It never failed to surprise her how weird people acted around her just because she was in the movies.

And then she'd sworn in front of him. She closed her eyes. Not being in the least religious, she'd never spoken personally to a priest, although he'd said he wasn't a priest but a deacon, whatever that was. He hadn't looked horrified, anyway. Hopefully she wasn't damned for all eternity just because she'd said the word shit.

Sighing, she turned off the shower, got out, dried herself, and pulled on a clean pair of cut-down jeans and a plain tee. After looking in the mirror, she reached for a wipe and carefully removed the last traces of mud, and most of her makeup. This was no place for six-inch-thick foundation and lipliner. She left her eyes, because without mascara it didn't look as if she had any eyelashes, but when she'd done she looked fresh-faced and several years younger. It seemed to fit with her return to the Northland, and the fact that she was staying with her childhood friend.

Going back into her bedroom, she took her phone out of her purse and sat on the bed with it. In the city, it was rarely out of her hand. She texted constantly, answered fans' emails, posted photos of wherever she was staying, and made sure her Facebook, Twitter, and Instagram accounts were all up-to-date. It was a huge part of her life, and yet, at that moment, she didn't want to turn it on. It was as if she'd had a radio tuned in between stations and had been listening to white noise for years, and suddenly she'd turned it off. The silence was deafening and had made her uneasy at first, but her heartbeat was gradually slowing, her sense of anxiety calming like a raging sea after the wind began to die down.

Now, though, as she turned on the phone again, her heart rate picked up, and her mouth went dry.

She had thirty-four unanswered texts, eleven missed phone calls, twenty-two emails, and numerous comments on her social media that she hadn't yet replied to. Her heart sinking, she scanned through the texts and emails. In the past, she would've been horrified and would have sat and answered them all immediately. As she scrolled down, though, she realized how few of them were important enough to demand an immediate reply. She didn't mean to belittle her fans, because she never took them for granted, but none of this stuff was life or death. None of it really mattered. Not in the big scheme of things, when her very sanity was hanging in the balance.

Taking her time, she listened to her phone messages. Two were from her mother, seven from her agent, and two were from journalists keen for her to tell her side of the 'Jack and Felicity' story.

Normally, she would have rung her agent first. Today, though, she called her mother.

"Fliss!" Annabel Rivers sounded a mixture of furious and relieved. "Where on earth are you? I've been worried sick."

"I turned my phone off about six hours ago, Mum. It's hardly long enough to declare a state of emergency."

"You just vanished without a word to anyone. Kurt has called me about three hundred times. He's out of his head with worry."

Fliss didn't say anything. Her agent was alarmed that she was going to turn down Whitfield's role, that was all. He didn't give a damn about how she was feeling.

Then she felt a twinge of shame. He'd been her agent for five years; he was bound to be concerned. This was his business. Her state of mind would be important to him, if only because it could impinge on the rest of her career.

"I'll call him in a minute," she said. "I just wanted to tell you I'm okay, and I'm taking a few days off."

"Off?" Annabel sounded bemused. "You're an actress, you can't take time off. Especially now. You need to get back here and sort out this mess with that fucking moron."

"I presume you're talking about Jack."

"Seriously, Fliss… You let him take photos of you?" Annabel sounded incredulous. "What were you thinking?"

Her eyes filled with tears. "I thought he loved me, Mum. I thought we were going to get married."

"At least you were wearing nice underwear in them."

Fliss said nothing.

"The rest of the photos are more of the same?" her mother asked.

"I think so." Fliss closed her eyes. He'd been so loving, telling her he had to take photos to capture her looking so beautiful. She'd believed every word he'd said.

"And what's this about a video?" her mother continued.

"I don't know anything about a video."

"What do you mean?"

"He filmed me without asking me."

"The fucking bastard. I'm going to rip off his fucking head and spit down his neck."

Fliss lay back on the bed and covered her face with her hand. "Mum…

"Why aren't you angry about this?"

"I am angry. I'm also upset and hurt."

"Jesus. You need to pull on your big girl pants and deal with this. What's the video of?"

"I don't know, I haven't seen it." The worst thing was that she had no idea.

"Jesus. You're so naive. Haven't I taught you anything? You never trust any man until that ring is on your finger, and not even then. Men can't be trusted. I've told you this over and over, but you never listen. You only have yourself to blame. You need to sort this out. This is slut shaming of the worst degree. Fucking men putting women down for their sexuality."

Fliss felt physically sick.

"What you're going to do," her mother continued, "is come home, put your face on, and get back out there with your chin held high. I told Kurt to book you a slot on Five Live tonight here in Wellington, so you can have a chance to tell your story, and—"

Fliss hung up.

Immediately, she regretted it. Annabel would be livid. The next time she called, she'd have to apologize, or she'd never hear the end of it.

Slowly, she brought up her agent's details and pressed the green button.

"Felicity!" Kurt blew out a sigh of relief. "Chickadee, I've been so worried. Are you all right?"

"No," Fliss said. A tear ran down her cheek. "I'm going away for a few days. I thought you should know."

Kurt was silent for a moment. Then he said, "This is the most important time in your career, honey. You're not the first actress to have something like this happen, and you won't be the last. But I've been in the business long enough to know how to handle it. You need to appear strong, and to tell your story and put that jackass in his place."

"I can't," she said. "Not right now."

"Jack's created a situation, and that's not going away whether you like it or not. You can't back down now, honey, or you'll be seen as weak. Women all over the world are waiting for you to get out there and say, 'I look amazing in those photos, and fuck you Jack, you've done me a favor'. You need to own this situation, honey, and fill that void, or the internet is going to fill it for you, and you don't want that, believe me."

"I can't," she repeated.

"Jesus." She could almost see him running his hand through his graying hair. "You think you're the only woman ever to be humiliated by a man? Do you really want people to think that you're ashamed of these photos?"

"I am ashamed of them," she said fiercely.

"You can't be," he snapped. "You need to hold your head high, and—"

"They were personal and private," she said, "and I thought I was sharing myself with a man who loved me. I feel humiliated and embarrassed and hurt, and I am not going on prime-time TV so that everyone can gawp at me as if I'm in a zoo."

"You need to—"

"I don't need to do anything. I rang you out of courtesy to let you know I'll be off the grid for a few days. I'll get back in touch when I've decided what I'm going to do. I'm sorry, Kurt, I know I'm letting you down, but I just can't deal with it right now." Her voice was husky, tears brimming in her eyes.

"All right," he said, obviously noticing her emotion. "Take a couple of days. But no longer than that. You call me on Sunday, okay?"

"I will. Thanks." She hung up, and then she turned off the phone and tossed it aside.

For a while, she just lay there, looking up at the ceiling, too tired and dispirited to move. Eventually, though, she pushed herself up and wandered along the corridor to find Roberta.

She was in the kitchen with Emily. Fliss leaned on the doorjamb, smiling in spite of herself at the sight of Roberta and her niece making bread at the large table in the middle of the room. Music was playing, and the two of them were singing while they kneaded the dough.

Emily had long brown hair and a pretty face with a snub nose. She didn't look much like Dominic. She must look like her mother. How sad that the girl had lost her mum at such a young age. And that Dominic had lost his wife. He must only be in his early thirties. That was no age to be widowed. Roberta had said his wife had died two years ago. Were deacons allowed to remarry? Was he dating anyone else? Fliss knew nothing about the rules and regulations of the Church. It made her a little uneasy knowing what he did. Had Roberta told him what had happened with Jack? She could only imagine that he'd look down on her for it.

She rested her head on the doorjamb, overwhelmed for a moment by sadness.

Roberta glanced up, saw her there, and smiled. "Hey."

Emily looked up too then. "Hello!"

"You must be Emily," Fliss said. "Nice to meet you."

"Nice to meet you, too. We're making bread!"

"So I see." She came into the kitchen and perched on one of the stools. "Is this for dinner?"

"We're having chicken casserole," Emily said, "and we thought we'd make some rolls to go with it."

"Sounds lovely."

"Emily wants to stay for dinner," Roberta said. "They usually do, but Dominic didn't want to intrude. We'll have to talk him into it."

Fliss hesitated. She could have done with a quiet evening this first night, just her and her friend alone to talk.

"You don't mind, do you?" Roberta asked. "I thought you'd like to catch up."

"Of course," she said politely. "It's just… I'm not sure I can cope with anyone being judgmental right now."

Roberta laughed. "Dominic is the least judgmental person you're likely to meet. He's a counselor at the high school. Don't be put off by the collar. He's not going to push his faith on you." She glanced at Emily, who was singing along to the music. "He didn't recognize you," she said softly.

"But you told him?" Fliss asked. Roberta nodded. Fliss swallowed. "Has he… seen the photo?"

"No."

"Do you think he'll look it up?"

Roberta gave her a mischievous smile. "Well, he may be a deacon, but he's a man, too. It'll be interesting to see if he does."

Fliss hoped he wouldn't, but she knew she probably would look, if she were him and had discovered what had happened. "What made him want to be a deacon?" Fliss asked.

"Jo played a big part," Roberta said, obviously not worried about mentioning Emily's mum in front of her. Fliss was rapidly realizing that Roberta said whatever was on her mind. It was quite refreshing not to have to worry about what someone was thinking.

"She was religious?" Fliss asked.

Roberta nodded, showing Emily how to stretch the dough with the heel of her hand, then fold it over. "He was very young when he met her—she was his first girlfriend. They married at twenty-one. Our parents are Anglican by birth, but our family's only ever gone to church for weddings and funerals. Jo was very religious though, and Dominic started going with her. He was already training to be a counselor, and when she suggested being a deacon, I guess it seemed like a natural progression for him, and a way to become more involved in the community."

"What is a deacon?"

"It's the first step to becoming a priest."

"How long has he been one?"

Roberta looked at Emily, who said, "Six years."

"And he's not going to be a priest?"

Roberta shook her head. "His faith is important to him, but it's his role in the community that's he loves. I think he knows every single person in the town, not just everyone who goes to church. I don't get it myself; I like being alone. I don't like crowds much. But Dominic sees all the pain out there, all those who are sick and struggling, and he feels some weird compulsion to help them."

"He sounds like a saint," Fliss said.

"Oh, he's not," Roberta replied fervently, and Emily shook her head in agreement.

"He's grumpy in the mornings," Emily said. "Until he has his coffee. And he can't cook. He burns everything. Even pizza."

"He writes terrible science fiction stories." Roberta started placing the rolls in a tin. "If he asks you to read them, make some excuse; they're awful."

"He kills plants," Emily said. "Mum used to say he had brown fingers, and she'd never let him water her tomatoes or strawberries because they'd be dead in a week."

Fliss started laughing. "Poor Dominic."

"But he can play the acoustic guitar like a diva," Roberta said. "And he really does have a gift with people. Everyone loves him."

"All right," Fliss said softly, "you've convinced me. We'll ask him to stay for dinner."

"Yay!" Emily jumped up and down. "Can I go and play with Jasmine now, Roberta?"

"Wash your hands, then of course you can."

Fliss smiled as the girl washed the flour off then went into the living room to play with the cat.

"She's lovely," she said, standing to dry the bowls and spoons as Roberta washed them up.

"Yeah, she's a sweetie." Roberta scrubbed at the mixing bowl.

"She's lucky to have you." Fliss took the bowl from her.

"Oh, we all look after her, Mum and the others. We try and help Dominic out. It's hard work being a single parent, especially when you're working."

"And can't cook."

Roberta laughed. "Yeah. So... how are you doing? You looked a bit pale when you came out of the bathroom."

"I've just rung Mum and my agent."

"Ah."

"Yeah. They want me to go home, obviously. But... I can't. Not yet." Fliss dried a wooden spoon and put it in the drawer.

"You don't have to," Roberta said. "Stay here as long as you like."

Fliss gave a soft laugh. "Thank you. You're very sweet."

"I think that's the first time I've ever been called that," Roberta said wryly. "Elliot would laugh his head off if he heard you."

"For someone who's just declared they don't like people, it's incredibly generous of you to offer me a place to stay."

"Well, you're not just anyone, are you?" Roberta sounded perfectly sincere. "Everyone needs to escape from time to time. I'm not Dominic, I'm no counselor, and I can be guaranteed to say the wrong thing at any given moment, but all I will say is that you shouldn't take shit from anyone. Your life is your own, not Jack Leeson's, not your mum's, not your agent's. The only person you have to please is yourself."

Fliss smiled at her, knowing it was pointless to try to explain that everyone in her life thought they had a stake in her career, like owning shares in a company. And everyone had their idea of what to do with it. She'd spent so long trying to please everyone else, she wasn't even sure what she wanted anymore.

Chapter Six

At around five thirty, Dominic pulled up outside Roberta's house again. It had been a busy afternoon, and he turned off the engine and sat there for a moment, letting the peace and quiet of the place seep into his bones. He was tired, and he was looking forward to getting home, having dinner, putting Emily to bed, and then having a soak in the spa with a glass of whisky. Quite often, Emily would come running out when she saw his car, and he'd have a quick word with Roberta through the car window without having to get out. But no Emily appeared today, so he was going to have to go in.

It would, of course, mean meeting Fliss Rivers again.

He scratched at a mark on the steering wheel, then angled the rear-view mirror down to check his hair.

On the way out of town, he'd slowed by the cinema to look at the poster of Fliss in *Love for a Lifetime*. He'd seen the way she stared up at her co-star lovingly, although of course she was an actress, so it was hard to tell if the adoration was genuine. Judging by her predicament, he suspected it might have been.

It was sad, how often relationships failed to work out. He'd been so lucky with Jo. They'd had their ups and downs, of course; no marriage was perfect, and there were times when they'd argued. She'd always been level headed, though, and it had been him who'd been the one to storm out and bang the door, only to return half an hour later with his tail between his legs to apologize.

He could feel her now, her dark eyes watching him as he checked his hair. "Just making sure I'm presentable," he mumbled, angling the mirror back up.

With a sigh, he got out of the car, went over to the front door, and let himself in. Voices echoed from the kitchen, so he walked through and discovered Emily sitting at the kitchen table with Roberta and Fliss, playing Rummy.

"Are you teaching my daughter to gamble?" He leaned against the door and slid his hands into his pockets. A small pile of twenty-cent coins sat in the middle of the table.

"Yep. She's won five bucks off me already." Roberta took a card and groaned. "I am so unlucky at this game."

"Only five bucks? I'd hope you'd win at least twenty. Then we could have a takeaway cheese-crust pizza for dinner." He smiled.

Emily took a card, laid down three jacks and four aces, and took the money in the middle as the two women groaned. "Roberta said we can stay for dinner."

"No," Dominic said. "That would be rude when Roberta has a guest."

"I don't mind." Fliss lifted her turquoise gaze to him. "It would be nice to catch up."

"We made bread," Emily protested.

Fliss held his gaze for a moment. Her hair was damp around her temples—she'd had a shower, and she must have taken off some of her makeup, because she looked about five years younger, fresh-faced, and beautiful.

He shouldn't stay. He had paperwork to do, and he'd been planning to make notes on some essays he'd been reading. And the spa and the whisky beckoned. The last thing he needed was to be distracted by some ditzy actress with long eyelashes.

Immediately, he felt ashamed. Fliss was in trouble, and she didn't deserve the label, even if she had fallen in the mud at his feet.

"All right," he said. "As long as you don't mind."

"Take the collar off, though," Roberta told him. "It's weirding Fliss out."

Fliss gave him an embarrassed look. "It's not."

"It really is," Roberta said. "She thinks you're going to call a plague of locusts on her every time she says shit." Emily giggled, and Roberta pulled an *eek* face. "Sorry."

His lips curving up, Dominic unbuttoned the collar at the back and left it on top of his keys. "Better?"

"If only the impeccably high moral standards could be discarded as quickly." Roberta winked at him, then rose and picked up the oven mitts to get the bread out of the oven.

Fliss stifled a laugh. "Don't you start," he scolded her, coming over to open the cupboard where Roberta kept the dishes. "I don't know what a man needs to do to get some respect around here nowadays."

Roberta grinned and began putting the rolls into a basket lined with a clean cloth. "So, what have you been up to this afternoon?"

He carried four dishes across to the table, where Emily was laying out the placemats. "I went to the hospice for a while. Then I made a couple of house calls."

"Mr. Peters?" Roberta asked, gesturing to Fliss to get some wine glasses and a bottle from the rack. When he nodded, she said, "How is he?"

He tipped his head from side to side. "He's an old schoolteacher," he explained to Fliss, shaking his head when she offered him a glass. He took a seat opposite her as she poured herself and his sister the wine. "He taught Roberta. His family live in Auckland, and his wife died a few years ago. And now he's got bowel cancer. He's finding it a bit tough to deal with."

"What do you do?" Fliss asked. "Do you listen to his confession and stuff like that?"

"Don't do much of that in the Anglican Church. And nothing as formal as that, anyway. Mostly I just keep an eye on people and see if I can help. I have a lot of contacts at the hospital, and at social services. So, if someone's not eating, for example, or having trouble getting to and from the hospital, I can organize meals-on-wheels or transport for them, and make sure they're being cared for. Sometimes, they just want someone to talk to."

Roberta put the basket of rolls in the middle, then brought over the crockpot and started ladling the casserole into their dishes.

"So, is that voluntary work?" Fliss asked, taking a roll, and splitting it down the middle.

Dominic did the same, scooping up some of the softened butter and smoothing it over the soft bread inside. "I get a stipend from the Church for community work, which enables me to work part time at the school." He took a bowl of the casserole from Roberta. "Wow, this smells amazing."

"God bless the crockpot," Roberta said cheerfully, taking her seat. "Dig in."

Dominic dipped his spoon in the casserole and took a mouthful. It was heavenly, his mouth filling with the taste of herbs and spices, the vegetables tender without being soft, the chicken cooked to perfection.

"We should get a crockpot," Emily said.

"It would stop you burning the pizza," Roberta added.

"Ha ha." He scowled and took a bite of the buttered roll. "I'm all about feeding the soul. I'd rather leave the stomach to someone else."

"You need a good woman to look after you," his sister suggested.

It wasn't the first time she'd suggested it was time for him to date again. He'd ignored her in the past, and he was happy to ignore her this time, too.

"I've been thinking about getting a housekeeper," he said.

Fliss gave a short laugh, and he sent her an amused look. She broke off a piece of her bread roll, her eyes dancing. "I hear you write science fiction novels. You'll have to let me read one of them." She popped the piece of roll in her mouth.

Emily pulled a face, and Roberta pursed her lips as he looked at her.

"I see," he said. "Been advising our guest of all my foibles, have we?"

"That would take all week," his sister replied.

He snorted and dug his fork into a piece of chicken. "I like writing—it's escapism. Doesn't mean I'm any good at it."

"But you play guitar," Fliss said, having a sip of her wine. "You'll definitely have to give me a demonstration of that later."

He chewed the chicken, glancing at his daughter, wondering what else they'd told Fliss about him. Emily just grinned at him and dug into her dinner. He sighed and ate his roll.

"Tell me about the Bay of Islands Brides," Fliss asked Roberta. "And all about your café. I was so impressed with your range of cakes and muffins."

"Oh, there's not a huge variety," Roberta said, but she looked pleased all the same. Dominic hid a smile and ate his dinner as his sister described the setting up of the bridal shop, how Phoebe and Bianca made the dresses, and their mother ran the place. Roberta was quick to discount her role in the business, but she'd worked as hard as the rest of them to get the place going.

They talked about this and that, carefully avoiding any conversation about Fliss's issues. She talked a little about life in LA, but mostly she asked questions about the Northland, about people they'd known when they were young, and places they'd frequented as kids. Dominic felt himself transported back to those days when it seemed as if the sun always shone, and there was nothing more serious to worry about than what homework was due and making sure he was fit for a rugby match at the weekend.

Fliss obviously felt the same, because she laughed a lot, putting aside her worries for a while. If nothing else, he thought, at least he and Roberta had been able to give her a short respite from her troubles, even if it was only postponing the inevitable.

When they finished dinner, they cleared away the dishes and then had a piece of Roberta's baked apple pie with vanilla ice cream.

"I haven't eaten so much in years," Fliss said when she'd finished, leaning back with a groan.

"Good," Roberta said. "You need some flesh on those skinny bones."

After that, the girls talked him into joining them for another game of Rummy, which turned into a tournament, and before he knew it, it was seven thirty and Emily was starting to yawn.

"I've got an idea," Roberta said when her niece protested as she tidied up the cards. "How about you have a bath here tonight? I've got some nice bubble bath you'll love, and then I'll braid your hair for you."

"Oh, can I Daddy?" Emily asked, jumping up and down.

"All right," he said good-naturedly, too full of casserole and apple pie to complain.

"We'll join you on the deck in a while," Roberta told them. "Dom, can you light the candles out there?"

"Okay." He grabbed a box of matches, and he and Fliss made their way into the living room and out through the sliding doors onto the deck. He lit the big candles that hung in glass bowls from the overhanging roof, casting pools of buttery light across the deck and surrounding them with the scent of citronella to keep away insects.

Picking up the guitar he left at Roberta's, he took one of the comfy chairs, propped his feet on the table in the middle, and tuned the guitar up. Fliss appeared, wrapped in a thick jumper against the evening breeze, and she put her wine on the table and curled up in the chair next to him.

He picked out an old Jack Johnson song, singing about the fruits lying on the ground and birds moving back into the attic, a song that always reminded him of autumn. Even in the sub-tropical Northland, the evenings were starting to cool. He could no longer hear cicadas in the trees, and the sun had set a couple of hours ago, so beyond the deck the garden faded into darkness. The chickens had long since gone home to roost, and not far from the house a morepork—a native owl—hooted in the bushes.

"Thank you for a lovely evening," Fliss said when he stopped singing.

Still playing, he brought his gaze back to her to see her watching him. "I just hope we haven't intruded. I'm sure the last thing you wanted when you agreed to stay here was to have dinner with an excitable seven-year-old and a chaplain."

She smiled. "I'll admit I was a bit nervous when I saw your collar. But in actual fact, you seem quite nice." Her eyes danced; she was teasing him.

"Well, obviously, I have the ear of the big man, so I'll put in a good word for you." He picked out a few notes of *The Lord is My Shepherd*, then stopped and smiled.

She sighed. "Actually, I'd appreciate that." She picked up her wine glass and leaned back, resting her head on a hand. "I envy you your faith. My family has never been religious. Roberta said your parents were Anglican?"

"Mum went to church as a kid, but stopped going in her teens," he said. "Dad continued to go sporadically until he died."

"I bet he was proud of you."

"I think so. He liked that Elliot and I help people. He thought that was important."

"What does Elliot do again?"

"He's a cop. And Phoebe's husband is a firefighter."

"All heroes," she said with a smile. "I played a doctor in *Shortland Street*. I thought then how nice it must be to help people on a daily basis. I don't quite get the same satisfaction being an actress." Her lips twisted.

Dominic slid down in the seat a little, stretching his legs as he strummed an old blues song. "You entertain people, help them forget their problems for a while. That's no small thing."

Her turquoise eyes surveyed him. "That's a nice thing to say."

He shrugged, looking down at the strings as he picked out some notes.

"Do you find the good in everyone?" she asked.

"I try. I might have trouble with your co-actor, though," he said wryly.

She looked into her wine glass. "You know what happened, then."

"Roberta told me. I didn't before."

"You hadn't read it in the news, or online?"

"Don't read gossip columns much."

She chewed her lip. "So… have you seen the photo?"

"No."

"You didn't look it up before you came here?" She lifted her gaze to his again.

He got the feeling this was some kind of test. "No," he repeated. "Why would I? It was supposed to be private." He held her gaze, and started strumming Aguilera's *Beautiful*, singing Costello's version.

Slowly, Fliss's lips curved up in a smile.

His heart picked up speed, and a tingle ran down his spine again like a cool warning finger.

Careful, Jo said in his head.

I know. But he wasn't doing anything inappropriate. He could see that Fliss needed to talk, and this was what he did for a living. This was work, nothing more.

Yeah, he thought as a light blush touched her cheeks. *You keep telling yourself that and maybe you'll believe it.*

Chapter Seven

Fliss sipped her wine and snuggled down a little more into her chair.

Dominic continued to play *Beautiful*, singing along to the words. Even though he didn't look at her again, she knew he was directing it at her, telling her not to let other people get her down, that she was better than that.

When he'd finished, he smiled at her, then put the guitar by the side of the chair.

"Roberta was right, you do play like a diva," she said.

His eyebrows rose. "She actually said something nice about me?"

"She adores you, Dominic. As does your daughter. It was nice to see."

He just smiled. Then he said, "I'm sorry to hear you're having a tough time."

She leaned her head on the back of the chair. "I only have myself to blame."

"Didn't sound that way to me."

"I should have been more careful. I let Jack take photos of me. I trusted him, and I should have known better."

Dominic pursed his lips. "I've always believed it's good to think the best of people and to trust your instincts. When someone else behaves badly, it's not our fault for not anticipating their behavior. He did you wrong, Fliss. He was your partner. You let him into your life in the most intimate of ways. For him to take advantage of that doesn't reflect well on him at all. It was the equivalent of a family member mugging you on the street and stealing your purse."

She swallowed hard. "My mother thinks I was naive."

"Mothers often have a degree in hindsight. It's what *you* think and feel that matters."

"Do you know," she said softly, "I think you're the first person ever to say that to me."

He shrugged. "Everyone thinks their opinion is the most important. But if you do what others say all the time and don't follow your heart, you're never going to be happy."

She looked out at the garden, at the vegetable patches lit by the candles, fading away gradually into darkness. "I could have done with that advice back when I was a teenager."

"What would you have done differently?"

"I don't know." The stars were popping out in the night sky, the Southern Cross clearly visible to the south. "I've asked myself that a lot lately. Would I still have been an actress? Maybe. I don't want you to think I'm not grateful for my life and what I've achieved. I give thanks every day—maybe not in a religious sense, but I do count my blessings. I feel as if I'm living to please other people at the moment, though, and it gets me down."

"It happens sometimes. People take us for granted, and we have to go through a period of shifting in our relationships, a jostling of the balance of power, before everything settles again."

"I know what you're saying, and I think you're right where relationships are concerned. But, I feel that I'm being… exploited, I suppose. And I don't know what to do about that. I don't know if I'm strong enough to deal with it."

"Are you talking about your ex?"

"No, actually. I mean my mother and my agent, and everyone else in the business. My mother tells everyone that I've wanted to be an actress since I was two, but sometimes I wonder if it was her dream and not mine, you know? I mean, I've enjoyed it, and worked damn hard at it. And I'm proud of what I've achieved. But right now, sitting here after everything that's happened, I'm not sure I want to do it anymore."

"That's tough," Dominic said. "Especially with such a big part looming."

"I know. I feel as if I'm standing at a crossroads. This role is everything I've ever wanted, and I know it's my one big chance, and I'd be stupid to pass up on it. I was so excited… and then this thing with Jack happened, and it all just went to shit. And now I don't know what I want or what to do."

"Did he post the photo because you broke up with him?"

She finished off her wine. "It was a combination of factors. What the papers won't tell you is that I broke up with him because he cheated on me."

Dominic stared at her, then gave a short, humorless laugh. "I see."

"Well, he didn't see it that way. A friend saw him kissing another actress at a party. I confronted him, and he said it was just a kiss and they didn't sleep together, and I was getting my panties in a twist about nothing. That's Hollywood, you know? But it broke my heart. I've had a few relationships and I really fell hard for this guy. We hadn't been dating long, but I thought he was The One. And he goes and kisses someone else. I think, if I'm honest, part of me deep down was having doubts about his feelings for me before this happened, and I suppose that's why I took it so hard. It felt as if he was cheating. And therein lies the difference, I guess. My mother and both my sisters said I was reading too much into it." She studied Dominic, who was watching her, something about his very presence making her feel calmer. "Do you think they were right?"

"Are you asking me as a man? Or me as a deacon?"

"Would the answer be different depending on which one I asked?"

He smiled. "Whole books have been written on the importance of intention in committing a sin. The answer must be whether the person who does the act knows it's going to cause offence to someone else. Would Jack have kissed this other woman in front of you? Of course not, because he'd have known it would upset you, and therefore he's culpable. He shouldn't have done it."

Fliss stared at him. "I think that's the best explanation I've ever heard."

"Makes sense to me."

"So that's the deacon talking. What would the man say?" She waited for him to make a joke about guys kissing whomever they felt like.

"Same," he said. "But I've only ever kissed one woman in my life, and probably will only ever kiss one woman, so I suppose I'm the wrong person to ask."

"Aw," she said, "you're only, what, thirty-two? You have plenty of time to meet someone else."

He scratched at a mark on his jeans. "I don't know that I could do that. I promised to love her forever."

"Until death do us part?" she said softly.

He gave her a strange look. "That's odd. Emily said those very words today."

She studied his face, seeing a flash of pain across his features. "Did that hurt?"

"Yeah. A bit. I thought Emily was going to say she never wanted another woman to replace her mother, but she said she wants me to remarry so she can be a bridesmaid again." His lips twisted.

"It's a bit of a drastic move just to get her a new dress," Fliss joked.

He smiled. "Well, I suppose I should get her home, it's nearly nine." He got to his feet.

"I think I'll have another glass," Fliss said, picking up her wine glass and walking in with him. "Don't judge me."

"Hey, the only reason I'm not drinking is because I have to drive home. Go for it."

"You're allowed to drink?" she asked.

He laughed. "I'm not the Archbishop of Canterbury. And I bet he enjoys a brandy, anyway." He paused by the bathroom, frowned, then walked on. Stopping in the doorway to Roberta's bedroom, he stared into it, then sighed and gave Fliss a wry look.

She walked up to join him and discovered Emily and Roberta both curled up in her bed under the covers, fast asleep, Jasmine the cat lying between them.

Dominic blew out a breath, pulled the door closed, and gestured with his head for Fliss to follow him back to the kitchen.

"You going to carry her to the car?" she asked.

He went over to a cupboard and took out a heavy-bottomed glass. "Nah. This happens a lot. I just kip in the spare room normally. But I'm happy on the sofa. I'll take her home in the morning." He picked out a bottle of whisky from the cupboard and then stopped and turned to her. "If that's okay?"

"Of course." She felt a little glow of pleasure knowing that they could carry on talking for a while. "So, you're a whisky man?"

"I like my Islay malts. They're an acquired taste." He tossed a couple of ice cubes into the glass and tipped an inch of whisky over the top. "Come on," he said, beckoning for her to follow him when she'd refilled her wine glass.

On the way, he picked a blanket up from the arm of the sofa. When they sat back in their chairs on the deck, he shook out the blanket and placed it over their legs, then leaned back with his glass. After taking a sip from the glass, he swallowed it and tipped his head back with a sigh. "*Aaahhh*. That's better."

Fliss's gaze lingered on the five o'clock shadow darkening his jaw, on his ruffled hair and half-lidded eyes. For a churchman, he was surprisingly sexy. It would be a crime if he stayed single for the rest of his life.

"The Church doesn't mind you drinking?" she asked, snuggling down.

"As long as I don't walk up the high street drunk as a skunk."

She laughed. "I can't imagine you doing that."

He smiled. "I took the role as deacon to be part of the community. It seems pointless to do the job if I'm not going to try to set an example."

"Don't you get bored being good all the time?" She sipped her wine, then laughed as he gave her a wry look.

"No time to get bored," he said.

"Do you get lonely?"

He had a big mouthful of whisky, holding her gaze, a mischievous twinkle in his eyes.

She started to laugh. "I wasn't thinking about sex."

"Oh, really?"

"I wasn't." Heat flooded her at the thought of sliding beneath the covers with this man. When he raised his eyebrows, she said, with mock exasperation, "Well, now I am!"

"Okay, so the answer to the question I'm sure you're dying to ask is no, I don't always have to do it in the missionary position." He chuckled, and she giggled.

"I shouldn't drink any more," she said, frowning into her wine.

He snorted. "You're in the middle of nowhere with a deacon. I think you're safe."

"Good point." She had another mouthful and sighed.

He leaned his head on a hand. "I'm sorry about your ex. Want me to go and punch his teeth down his throat?"

"I'd pay to see you do it wearing your dog collar." She grinned. "Have you ever hit anyone?"

"No. I'm a lover not a fighter."

That made her laugh.

"I hope we can help you find the answers," he said.

"You've already helped more than you could know."

"What are you going to do?"

"I don't know." She ran her finger around the rim of the glass, looking into the ruby red wine. "My mother and my agent think I need to call Jack's bluff and get out there with my head held high. They think I should be defending women against the slut shaming that keeps happening."

"That's very noble," Dominic said, "especially when it's not your private photos being splashed over the internet."

She gave him a grateful look. "You don't think I'm mad for being reluctant to do that?"

"I think that nobody has the right to tell you how to feel."

She liked the way he spoke so matter-of-factly. No wonder he was so well respected in his community. "Do you think I was naive? For letting Jack take those photos?"

He sipped his whisky. "I wouldn't dream of judging you because I don't know the circumstances. For example, I had a girl in my office today, sixteen years old, who told me she thought she was pregnant. It would have been the easiest thing to demand to know why she hadn't used condoms, to berate her for being dumb. But there are a thousand factors involved in her decision making. Maybe she'd never been taught the importance of condoms—she was away that day in sex ed class, or she just didn't understand. Perhaps she wanted to use them and he didn't, and he persuaded her to have sex without them. Maybe she did use one and it split or something. It's easy to be judgmental and to say, 'you should have done this', but as I said earlier, things are always easier with hindsight. People come to me often because they're in trouble. They don't need a lecture about the things they could've done better. They need help to put it right."

"Roberta said you were the least judgmental person I was likely to meet. I have to say I found that hard to believe, especially with your job, but I'm beginning to think she was right."

"I don't believe that having faith makes me superior in any way. I don't think God's going to give me premium seating on the cloud when I die. Although I like that idea. Gold La-Z-Boy armchairs with cup holders and a button you can press to strike lightning on the unfortunate down below."

"And a never-ending supply of chocolate.'

"Hey, if there ain't chocolate in heaven, I ain't going."

She laughed.

"In general, people are very quick to judge," he said. "I guess I was the same when I was younger. Now, though, I try not to make assumptions. No two people are alike, and it's wrong to accuse someone of being weak, for example, because they can't stand up for themselves, when you don't know their background. It's easier to be strong and confident when you come from a loving home and nobody's ever screwed you over. It's harder when every guy you've ever met has treated you badly, or when you've been mugged, beaten, or raped."

"True," she said. "I've never thought of it like that."

"And even then," he continued, "an event can make one person react one way, and another person in a completely different way. Even twins like Bianca and Phoebe, who were brought up the same, have different personalities and will have different reactions to situations. And who am I to judge them or anyone else? Like the girl who thought she was pregnant—I'm a white male who met the love of his life at eighteen and married her at twenty-one. Life has been good to me. How can I possibly understand the difficulties of being a young girl whose mother died when she was seven, who doesn't get on with her stepmother, and who's run away from home several times? The young man she met might have been the first person who has shown her attention in many years. Who made her feel wanted, even for a brief moment. I'm not going to look down on her for trying to find comfort and love wherever she can."

Chapter Eight

Dominic finished off his whisky, pushed the blanket to the side, and got to his feet. "I'm going to get another drink. You want another glass of wine?"

She sucked her bottom lip for a moment. "Can I have a whisky?"

He raised his eyebrows. "You like a malt?"

"I don't mind, and I'm in the mood for something a bit stronger."

"I'll get you a glass." He went inside and through to the kitchen, popped some ice into two glasses, and poured over a generous amount of amber liquid from the bottle of Lagavulin.

Then he stopped for a moment, leaned against the worktop, and had a mouthful of the whisky as he looked out into the night.

Jo had hated the peaty smell of the Islay malts with their strong aromas of brine and iodine. "You smell like a pharmacy," she'd complained once, pushing him away with a laugh when he'd tried to kiss her after having a drink.

I'm having trouble remembering her. His throat tightened at the thought that his daughter was beginning to forget her mother. But if he was honest with himself, Jo was fading in his memory, too. Some memories were bright and clear, and he could remember her long brown hair, her hazel eyes, the mole on her hip he'd kissed many times. But when he tried to picture her face, he received a blurred image, like a camera that was out of focus.

I'll never forget you, he whispered fiercely to the night sky. But the answer was silence, dark and empty, leaving him with a hollow feeling in the pit of his stomach and an ache in his heart. She'd never let him down in life, not once. She'd been solid as a rock, loyal, always there when he needed her. He was the one who'd been less than perfect on so many occasions, but he'd tried hard to do his best, to live up to her example. And yet, she'd left him, and for two years he'd been drifting, struggling to keep his head above water, missing her, and wondering how he was going to make it through the next day, let alone the next year.

He looked at the two glasses he was holding. A deep guilt gripped him at the thought that he was sitting with another woman, sharing an intimate moment with her. He could deny it all he liked, but it was the first time since Jo had died that he'd spent time alone in another woman's company, other than his mother or sisters, that wasn't related to work. It was the first time he'd gotten that feeling—the tingle down the spine, stir of the hibernating bear kind of feeling.

Well, it didn't matter what he was feeling, because Fliss was only here for a few days, and then she'd be returning to the city and heading off to LA or London or wherever she was filming. She was used to parties and rich guys in tuxedos. She was hardly going to be turned on by a Church deacon whose exciting events of the day including counselling a pregnant teen and comforting a dying pensioner.

With a sigh, he carried the drinks back outside, took his seat, and pulled the blanket over his legs. Fliss was still curled in her seat, and her green eyes shone in the light of the flickering candles.

"You're not getting too cold?" he asked her, passing her the glass.

She sniffed the whisky cautiously, then took a sip. To his pleasure, she didn't shudder or exclaim her disgust. She just murmured, "Mm. No. It's nice out here. It's so rarely quiet in the city. There are always sirens or car alarms or people shouting. Here… there's nothing. I can't tell you what a relief it is."

They sat for a while, sipping their whisky, letting the peace of the evening settle over them. When Roberta had told him that Fliss was an actress, he'd expected her to be talking non-stop, to be full of gossip, and to find the countryside terribly boring. Instead, although she was obviously torn up about her problems, she seemed delightful.

"I was just thinking how different my life would have been if I'd fallen for a man like you," Fliss said, taking him by surprise. Her lips curved up as his eyebrows rose. "I'm not coming on to you, by the way," she added. "I'm not so drunk that I'd chat up a churchman."

He chuckled, wondering what he'd have said if she hadn't added the disclaimer. "The thought never entered my head."

"It's just that my life has always been about drama. If something can be taken the wrong way, it is. It's fashionable to be offended by everything. And it's so relaxing being with someone who doesn't seem to be like that."

"You sound tired of the high life," he teased.

But she didn't smile. "I am. I have been for a while. Don't get me wrong, it was fun when I was younger, but lately it's lost its appeal."

"You're hardly old," he scoffed.

"I am in the business. I've started to age, Dominic, and I hate that it scares me. As an actress, every little line is to be feared. And I hate that. Growing older should be something to celebrate, but it's seen as a curse in Hollywood."

He studied her face, unable to find any lines on her smooth, pale skin. But that didn't mean they weren't there. He knew what she meant. Gray hairs and wrinkles were part of everyday life for most people, but she wouldn't be the only person in the world who hated the ageing process.

"I like being older," he said. "There's pressure on you when you're young to be fashionable, fit, and sociable. I like that I can be what I want to be now without worrying what anyone else thinks. I can be grouchy and bad-tempered and cantankerous and put it down to my age."

She giggled and sipped her whisky. "I doubt you're any of those things. But I envy you that freedom."

"What are you going to do about your ex?" he asked.

She bit her lip. "I don't know."

"Are you angry with him?" He was curious, because she didn't seem angry.

"Yes. I'm furious with him. With myself. With everyone who's trying to stick their oar in. I'm also embarrassed. And sad, and upset, and hurt. I'm excited about the new movie and now fearful I won't get it. I'm exasperated and bored and tired with the way the business is such a rollercoaster. It's all so superficial—everything is about how things look and appear rather than how they actually are, does that make sense? My emotions are a jumble, like a ball of knotted wool, and I can't separate them." She took a deep breath and blew it out slowly.

"You don't have to work it all out tonight," he said gently.

"No, I suppose not." She had a big mouthful of whisky, then coughed. "Anyway, enough about me. I'm bored with the subject. Let's talk about you. Should I call you Reverend?"

"Well, reverend is a description like honorable or venerable, so technically it's not right to call someone reverend—you wouldn't say, 'Hello, honorable.' My full title is The Reverend Dominic Goldsmith,

or Deacon Dominic, although a lot of people call me Deacon Dom."
He smiled. "You can just call me Dominic or Dom."

"How about Father?" she said impishly. "Should I call you that?"

"Not unless you have a daddy fetish." He blinked. "Sorry, did I say
that out loud?"

That made her laugh. "It would go with the Dom title too, I
suppose."

His lips curved up.

"I have a feeling the good guy image is just a cover," she said softly.

"Nah. I'm very dull." He held her gaze, still smiling.

"Do you wear your collar most of the time?" she asked.

"The bishop likes us to wear it when we're out in the community.
The school prefers me not to and I'm fine with that, because of course
here we have separation of Church and State—we don't teach religion
in schools. Plus, talking to a member of the clergy can put kids off,
whether they're religious or not. And I don't wear it when I'm with
friends and family. But I put it on when I go to the hospice, or the
hospital, or when I'm doing my calls, so people recognize me."

"But you're not going to be a priest?"

He shook his head. "All priests are deacons. Usually deacons are
ordained priests after a year. But I chose not to be. I'll stay as a deacon
for the rest of my life."

"Why didn't you want to be a priest?"

He inhaled and blew out the breath slowly. "I was already having
doubts, and then Jo—my wife—died. That kind of did it for me."

"Did it shake your faith?"

He tipped his head from side to side. "Not shake it, but it shifted
the emphasis, if you like. I go to church because I like seeing the
people, talking to them, helping them. I enjoy working in the
community, and I'm happy to continue to do so without carrying the
extra weight of the religious side of things. I've had a long talk to the
bishop about it, and he's happy for me to continue serving in the
community."

Fliss's cool eyes studied him. "It must have been very hard for you.
Losing your wife. I'm so sorry."

"It was. She was two weeks off turning thirty. It's no age."

"And there's me complaining about wrinkles and stupid photos,"
Fliss said, frowning. "How shallow of me. I'm so sorry."

He just smiled. "It's all relative. My pain is nothing compared to someone who's lost their whole family in a natural disaster, but that doesn't mean it doesn't hurt, and it's the same for you."

"Yes, but it's easy to get caught up in thinking that the world's coming to an end when really, nothing terrible has happened in the big scheme of things."

"That's true."

"Drama again," she said. "I'm the original Drama Queen."

He chuckled. "You don't strike me as being overly dramatic. But then I'm not seeing you in your natural habitat, I suppose."

"Oh, I'm not particularly loud, or gregarious, for that matter. I suppose I'm talking more emotionally. It's easy to ramp everything up so it all seems terribly desperate and end-of-the-world when everyone does the same around you. Obviously, having a photo published on the internet is nothing compared to losing your partner, or having your home destroyed in an earthquake or something. It's good to get it in perspective."

He nodded. "I can see that."

"So… you really don't think you'll ever marry again?"

He looked out into the darkness. "When she was dying, I promised her I'd never love anyone else."

Fliss didn't say anything for a moment, and he listened to the morepork hooting in the trees.

"That's a sweet thing to say," she said eventually.

He brought his gaze back to her. "I meant it."

"I know."

"At the time." The words were out before he could stop them. He cursed under his breath and looked out at the night again.

"Relationships are hard," she said. "I'm sure nobody goes into marriage planning to get divorced. Everyone swears 'till death do us part' but it's rare that a couple manages to fulfil that promise. You did, and that's wonderful."

He finished off his whisky. "But now I should move on?"

"I'm not saying that at all. I think it's rare to experience the kind of love that you had even once in a lifetime, and I can understand how you'd want to hold onto that, and why you'd feel as if you were betraying her by loving someone else. I suppose I'd just say that life is hard, and it brings us comfort to share it with someone else. Loving another woman wouldn't be a betrayal, Dominic, because loving someone else doesn't mean that you love the first person any less. Love is a wonderful gift, and any woman would be incredibly lucky to be loved by you, even if she knew she'd never hold that precious place in your heart."

Emotion welled up inside him, and he swallowed hard, blinking a few times, surprised by the effect her words had. Friends and family had told him his vow to Jo was honorable but dumb, for want of a better word. Roberta and the others had tried several times to convince him it was time to move on, and he'd been unable to describe how upset that notion had made him. Fliss was the first one to suggest it was possible to love again without losing the depth of love he had for his first wife. He was so taken aback, he could barely speak.

Even though she must have seen his emotion, she didn't apologize, just gave a small smile, and finished off her whisky. "Oh well. I suppose I should go to bed."

"How long are you here for?" he managed to say.

"Just a few days. Any longer and my agent might physically explode. I might go and help Roberta in the shop tomorrow morning." She ran the tip of her tongue around her lips, presumably removing the remnants of any drops of whisky, although it made Dominic's heart beat a little faster. "What are you up to?"

"It's the autumn fair at the primary school," he said. "I'm supervising the hospice's stall, selling items for their charity shop."

Fliss smiled. "I remember the autumn fair. Oh, I'd love to go. Maybe I'll walk over after I finish at the bridal shop."

"I'll look out for you," he said, pleased that he'd be able to see her again.

She held his gaze then, the candlelight flickering in her eyes. "Thank you for talking to me this evening."

"I'm sure I wasn't what you expected. Roberta would have been a better confidante."

"It's been lovely," she said. She stood and leaned toward him. Then she pressed a kiss to his cheek. "Goodnight."

Dominic watched her walk away. She glanced over her shoulder briefly before she disappeared down the corridor, the smile still on her lips.

He blew out a long breath, then rose and went into the kitchen to get another whisky. Returning to the deck, he sat in the chair, feet propped on the table, head resting on the back of the seat, and listened to the morepork hooting in the trees.

Chapter Nine

The following day, Fliss woke naturally for the first time in years. How strange not to be roused by the insistent beep of the alarm clock! She lay in bed for a moment, seeing the sun streaming through the curtains, and thought how different her day would have been if she was in LA. She would have risen while it was still dark to do her workout on the treadmill, showered, had a poached egg on a slice of toast, then got going, whether it was off to the studio or to her agent's or into the city for a meeting.

She stretched, then got out of bed, pulled on her robe, and visited the bathroom. She checked her appearance in the mirror. Not too bad. She brushed her hair and tied it in a messy bun, then made her way to the kitchen.

Roberta stood at the stove, frying bacon. There was no sign of Dominic or his daughter. Fliss glanced at the living room and saw the pillow and blanket he must have borrowed piled neatly on the arm of the sofa.

"Morning," she said, coming into the room.

Roberta glanced over her shoulder. "Morning!"

"Sorry I slept in."

"It's seven o'clock. On a Saturday."

"Like I said, sorry I slept in."

Roberta laughed. "The life of the rich and famous, eh?"

"I have to say, it's quickly losing its appeal when I see how the other half lives." Fliss went over to the coffee machine. "Can I make myself one?"

"Of course. Help yourself."

Fliss slotted a capsule into the machine, checked the water, and pressed the button to heat it up. "No Dominic this morning?"

"He left early—he's helping to set up the fair today, so they're pretty busy."

"I thought I might wander over there later," Fliss said innocently. "See the old school again." She waited for Roberta to give her a sly look and tease her about wanting to see Dominic, but she didn't. She just smiled and said, "Why not? There's always something lovely about the school fairs, all the homemade cakes and pickles, the lucky dips, the bouncy castles. Makes me broody though." She laughed.

"You want kids then?" Fliss carried her coffee to the kitchen table.

"Dunno really. I guess." Roberta dished up the bacon onto waiting slices of bread. "I don't *not* want them. I can't imagine what kind of mother I'd be. I'm too selfish to think about someone else all the time."

"Bullshit," Fliss said with a snort. "I can just see you making cookies here with your son or teaching your daughter how to sew."

"Maybe." She brought the bacon sandwiches over to the table, then went back to retrieve a bottle of ketchup. "How about you?"

Fliss studied the bacon sandwich, chewing her lip. It was at least four hundred calories. But it smelled wonderful. Fuck it. She picked it up and took a bite, closing her eyes as she chewed. Then she swallowed and sighed. "I don't know if marriage and kids are on the cards for me. At the moment, definitely not."

"Not surprising, after what's happened." Roberta sipped her coffee. "I'm sorry about last night, by the way. I fully meant to have a long talking session, but I just crashed out."

"Oh, don't worry. It was nice to catch up with Dominic. He's a good guy."

"The best. He's still amazingly good natured considering life fucked him over."

"Yeah, he talked a bit about his wife. He misses her." Fliss picked out a piece of bacon. "What was she like?"

"Jo? She was sweet. Everyone loved her. I found her a bit..." Roberta pursed her lips as she tried to find the right word. "Perfect, I suppose. She worked at the hospice, and she raised money for charity, and she was an amazing cook, and she was probably great in bed. You know the sort."

"Bitch," Fliss said, then grinned.

Roberta laughed. "Yeah, nah, she was nice enough. But us mere mortals didn't stand a chance. I think Dom struggled sometimes to keep up with her. He would have liked to have just put his feet up on a Sunday and watch TV or chill out with her, but she always pushed him to get out into the community. She wanted to go to Africa, did he tell you that? Be some kind of missionary out there. He told me they quarreled about that. I think it was the one time he put his foot down and said no. He didn't want to drag Emily around the world, and he loves his job here. Plus, although he's never said anything, I think he was conscious that she wanted to do these things because they made her feel a bit... superior, you know? Doing good deeds made her feel better about herself, and he's never been like that. He was mischievous when he was young and got into trouble sometimes. Elliot teases him mercilessly now about his holier-than-thou behavior. He loves to remind him of the times the two of them got into trouble in their teens."

Fliss smiled. "Do you think he'll ever get married again?"

"Maybe, if he finds the right woman. He's not even dated since Jo died. I know he worries about what his parishioners will think. Without sounding all nineteenth century, he has a reputation to uphold, and he can't just go around jumping in and out of bed with every woman he meets." Roberta took a big bite out of her sandwich.

Fliss did the same, wondering if that was a subtle warning. But Roberta smiled and nodded at the sandwich and said, "Okay?"

"It's lovely. I haven't eaten anything like this in years."

"I figured I needed to get some calories into you. I've seen more fat on a chicken nugget."

Fliss laughed. "Yeah, well. The camera adds ten pounds, so I can't afford to overeat."

"That sucks. I wouldn't make a good actress." Roberta finished off her sandwich and pushed it away. "I'll wash up, and then I was thinking... I normally go for a walk before I go to work. Would you like to come with me? We can have a chat while we walk, and you can tell me all about what's going on."

"That sounds great."

So, they washed up the breakfast things, pulled on some track pants and T-shirts, and then headed out of the house.

The road was quiet, with only the occasional passing car. The gently rolling hills of Waimate North glistened in the morning sunshine. Fliss breathed in the fresh country air and began to talk, telling Roberta all about Jack and what had happened, about the business, her life, and how constricted she felt, hemmed in by the pressures of maintaining her image.

"It doesn't surprise me that your mum is still a pain in the arse," Roberta said. "She always was a dragon."

Fliss gave a wry smile, watching two horses galloping around a field just for the sheer enjoyment of the day. "She's not all bad. I've needed her behind me, because there have been many times when I would have given up if it wasn't for her encouragement and support. It's not as if she had to drag me kicking and screaming to auditions when I was younger. I had stars in my eyes; I wanted to be famous. I can't blame her completely. I don't know what's changed. I've grown up, I suppose, and I'm finally seeing the business for what it is, and finding it wanting."

"A crisis of the soul?"

"Maybe. I said to Dominic last night that I envy him his faith. I'd like to believe in something other than how important it is to be trending on Twitter. I want to have conversations other than about who's sleeping with whom."

"Oh, we talk about that here, too," Roberta said. "Small communities are the worst."

"I guess. Maybe I'm looking for something that doesn't exist."

"No, I know what you mean. It happens to us all at some stage. We're both heading toward thirty—you're twenty-nine this year too, right? Our body clocks are ticking away. Half the time we can ignore it because we know we're still young and we're not even halfway through our lives. So, we play the field and concentrate on our careers and think we'll worry about it later. And then suddenly we think, oh shit, what if I wait and wait and then discover that I can't have kids? Or I don't find Mr. Right? What will I do then?"

Fliss didn't reply, and they walked in silence for a while. Roberta understood, Fliss thought. Maybe every woman of their age understood that conflict.

"Do you think Jack is going to release the rest of the photos, and the video?" Roberta asked.

"Yes. I can't believe he'll turn down the money. And he wants to hurt me."

"For ending the relationship?"

"For getting the part in Whitfield's movie. Probably getting the part. I'm sure he wants to try to sabotage that, if he can."

"What a fucking bastard."

"Yeah. That sums him up."

"What are you going to do?" Roberta asked as they neared the house.

"I don't know. I know what I should do—walk out with my head high, curse the world for its slut shaming, say I'm proud of those photos and that sex is nothing to be ashamed of, tell the world to go fuck itself, walk up to Whitfield and lift my chin and tell him I'm perfect for the role, and never, ever look back. In five years I could be up there with the top starlets earning a fortune."

They walked slowly up the drive to the house. "That's one option," Roberta said. "What's the other?"

"I walk away. From Jack, from the movie, from the whole business. Retire. Move to the boondocks and crochet blankets."

"I've got some great patterns," Roberta said, and they both started laughing.

"You make me feel better," Fliss said, stopping outside the house. "You make me feel... normal. You remind me of the importance of living in the real world, not just online. Do you know, I don't have my phone on me? It's the first time in, well, forever, that I've gone out without it. It's my lifeline, normally. I'm always on, checking Twitter, emails, calling people. And it feels really odd to realize there's a whole world out there that's not made out of pixels."

Roberta unlocked the front door and they went in. "I know what you mean. I went to Auckland Zoo once and took hundreds of photos and videos of the animals, putting them on Instagram and Facebook. And it was only later that I realized I'd spent the whole day looking at the world through my phone. I hadn't *seen* anything. It was quite a revelation—it shocked me. I still have my phone, of course, I'm not Jane Austen or anything, but since then I've tried to live in the real world a bit more."

Fliss went in, thinking how true that was. "Even when I was with Jack, he was just as bad, always texting, taking photos. I can't tell you how refreshing it was to talk to Dominic last night. He didn't get his phone out once."

"I'm not even sure he has one."

Fliss's eyes boggled. "Seriously?"

"Nah." Roberta grinned. "He does, and he's on Facebook, I think, but he doesn't go on Twitter or anything else, and I don't think I've ever seen him take a photo. He's very much a man of the real world."

She gestured toward the bathroom. "You have a shower first, if you like. And then when I'm done, we'll head out."

Fliss showered, re-tied her hair in a messy bun, did her makeup simply, and chose jeans and a simple pink top, bearing in mind she was heading off to the school fair later. As she dressed, she thought about what Roberta had said—that Dominic was a man of the real world. He would have no interest in the bedroom exploits of Hollywood starlets, or in attending cocktail parties or movie premieres. It would be strange to be with a man like that, who didn't spend all evening staring at his phone, but who looked at her instead, not in the way that men looked at her in the business, as an actress who needed to be ticked off their list. But in the way he had last night, with interest, maybe even with admiration and a touch of longing.

She was tired of men who wanted to use her as a stepping stone to stardom, who wanted to boast to their friends about how they'd managed to score the famous Felicity Rivers. And she was tired of the shallowness of Hollywood, of the drama, of the virtue signifying and people pretending to care about an issue because it made them look good rather than out of any heartfelt concern.

Dominic wasn't standing on a soapbox lecturing everyone about the rights of women or the plight of the homeless or the abysmal nature of child poverty, then going home feeling as if he'd done a good day's work. Maybe that's what his wife hadn't understood. Roberta had said that Jo had enjoyed feeling superior, and that she wanted to save the world because it made her feel better. But Dominic just wanted to help people one at a time, real people with real problems, and try to make their lives a little easier. To be there when they didn't have anyone else. His clerical collar was a symbol, that was all, for a deep love for his fellow human beings.

Boy, if that wasn't something to warm a girl's heart.

Chapter Ten

Gray clouds curled on the horizon, threatening the arrival of rain, but to Dominic's relief they drew no nearer, and Saturday afternoon proved to be bright and sunny.

The autumn fair was in full swing. Most of the primary school attended with their *whanau* or family, and there was also a good turnout from the rest of the community. There were loads of activities for the kids, from bouncy castles to donkey rides to magic shows, and in this relatively safe environment where everyone knew everyone else, kids could be left to play while the adults chatted by the food stalls and had roasted pork buns with apple sauce, sausage sizzles with fried onions, and a variety of cakes.

Dominic's stall was going well, and he'd already sold two-thirds of the items from the hospice charity shop. He'd spent most of the morning finishing off wrapping toys and other small items into packages for a lucky dip, and he was enjoying watching kids of all ages paying their dollar, picking a toy out of the barrel, then going over to their friends and family to swap it for something they really wanted.

Emily was off somewhere playing with her friends, although she appeared every thirty minutes or so with a request for food, drink, or change for some activity she fancied. But although he'd been abandoned, he was never short of company. There was always somebody stopping by to talk to him, whether it was another parent or someone from the town.

He kept one eye out for Fliss, although he didn't really expect her to turn up. He suspected her promise to come had been said out of politeness, as he couldn't possibly imagine what fascination a rural fair in a muddy field with pin-the-tail-on-the-donkey competitions and guess-the-number-of-jelly-beans-in-the-jar would hold for a movie star.

But just after two p.m., about halfway through the fair, he was in the middle of talking to one of his parishioners when out of the corner of his eye he saw Fliss waiting patiently for him to finish his conversation.

"Oh," he said, momentarily distracted. She wore jeans and a pretty pink top, and even though she had a hat and sunglasses, presumably in an attempt to remain inconspicuous, she radiated beauty.

"Friend of yours?" Mrs. Haggett asked with a touch of disapproval.

He cleared his throat. "Of my sister's actually. This is Fliss. Fliss, this is Mrs. Haggett."

"Lovely to meet you, dear," Mrs. Haggett said, her tone implying she was anything but pleased.

"Likewise," Fliss replied politely.

"You came," Dominic said with a smile.

"Wouldn't have missed it for the world." She slid off her sunglasses and met his gaze, and his heartbeat sped up despite him telling himself that she'd come to see her old school, not to see him.

Mrs. Haggett moved on, clearly not impressed by the local deacon chatting up a pretty blonde. "Sorry," he said, but Fliss just grinned.

"I guess she thinks I'm leading you astray."

He gave a wry smile and went to answer but held back the words as the stepfather of Emily's friend Kaia walked up.

"You've been here a couple of hours," Wiremu said. "Would you like me to take over for a while, so you can go and get something to eat?"

"That would be great, thanks." He handed over the money bag, trying not to smile as Wiremu's eyes twinkled. Slowly, he and Fliss began to walk around the stalls.

"Sorry I missed you this morning," he said. "I had to get going as I had lots of toys to wrap."

She laughed. "That's fine. I had a lie-in. First time in years!"

"I'm glad to hear it." She looked better this morning, the shadows beneath her eyes a little less dark.

"So, you're Deacon Dom today," she teased, glancing at his clerical collar.

He shrugged. "People like to see it, and I don't mind wearing it." He touched his fingers to it, suddenly self-conscious. "Does it make you uncomfortable?"

"Of course not! It... suits you." She lifted her gaze to him, and a touch of color appeared in her cheeks as she looked away.

He lowered his hand, his lips curving up, but didn't comment on it. "So, does any of this look familiar?"

"More than you'd think, actually." She gestured around the school buildings as they crossed the playground, carefully avoiding the line of kids waiting for the bouncy castle. "The central block is the same. That was my first classroom there." She pointed to the one at the end. "Mrs. Stride. I'll never forget her. Old dragon."

He chuckled. "She used to make Roberta cry."

"She made us both cry. At the same time. I think we were talking in class when we shouldn't have been."

"That figures."

She bumped her arm against his. "How rude."

"Sorry," he said, not meaning it, liking the brief contact. "But I'd never be surprised to hear Roberta being told off for talking."

She grinned. "I had a nice morning in the shop."

"Oh, really?"

"Your mother gave me a tour of the shop and the workroom, and I met Bianca and Phoebe. Bianca has just finished a new dress and Phoebe was planning out the embroidery. I don't know how she does it—I'm all fingers and thumbs when it comes to sewing."

"I'm so glad she stayed here in Kerikeri," he confessed. "Roberta told you about what happened to her, right? With the accident?"

"Oh yes, how awful for her and for you all."

"It was a tough time, especially for her husband."

"I haven't met him yet."

He'd been thinking about asking her something, and he decided to take the plunge. "Well, I don't know if Roberta's mentioned it to you, but Mum's having a get-together tomorrow. We're having a barbecue and most of us will be there. Of course, you came here for peace and quiet, so I understand if you'd rather not, but—"

"I'd love to come," she said.

He smiled. "Okay."

They walked a little in silence, although it wasn't because he couldn't think of anything to say. He had nothing in common with this woman other than that they'd been brought up in the same small town, and their worlds couldn't have been more different. He'd known her for just twenty-four hours. And yet he felt a connection with her he couldn't explain.

"Daddy!" Emily came running across the playground to see him with one of her friends. "Oh, hello," she said as she saw Fliss. Dominic watched her nudge her friend Kaia, who giggled.

"Hello," Fliss said. "Are you enjoying the fair?"

"It's brilliant. Dad, can I have some more change for the go-karts? *Pleeeeease.*"

"Okay," he said good-naturedly, fishing out some coins.

"Thanks." Emily took them and ran off, her friend close behind.

"She seems to be having a good time." Fliss fell into step beside him as they reached the bottom of the playground and turned to head back.

"She loves it here. I'm lucky that she enjoys going to school. I know from my job that it's not the same for every kid."

"I keep forgetting you're a school counselor. You're at the high school though, right?"

"Yes."

"Of course you are, you mentioned dealing with a teen pregnancy the other day. Does that happen a lot?"

"Not a lot. Once or twice a year, maybe. Sometimes they're just worried they might be pregnant, which is what happened in this case. Even these days when kids are relatively switched on, and they all have sex ed classes unless their parent specifically asks them to be removed, you still get confusion as to the technical details."

"It's funny," she said, "I never considered that you might have to counsel that sort of thing."

"Neither did I when I started the job. Elliot thinks it's hilarious."

She chuckled. "What was the problem with the teen you saw yesterday?"

"They didn't use a condom. Her boyfriend told her she couldn't get pregnant the first time, especially if he didn't... um..." He cleared his throat. "...come inside her, but her friend told her she could and made her panic. These kids know the basics, but a lot of the little details escape them."

"And so you have to put them straight?"

"In this case, I sent her over to the nurse for a pregnancy test. I couldn't face sex ed last thing on a Friday."

They both laughed.

"Seriously, though," he said, waving to one of his parishioners as they passed a stall selling hot sausage rolls and pies, "it got me thinking about Emily, and how I should really have a sit-down talk with her about all this sort of stuff. I'd hate for her to be as clueless as that teenager."

"That's hard for you. I suppose it's usually the mother who has the chat with daughters. It was in our family."

"Yes, of course, Jo would have had it all sorted by now."

It felt odd, saying his wife's name to Fliss. It made him feel uncomfortable, as if he was being disloyal by spending time in the company of another woman. But he wasn't cheating on her or anything. They were just walking and talking. They weren't even touching.

Then he felt a twinge of guilt. Hadn't he said to Fliss that intention was everything? That sin occurs when a person commits an act knowing it's going to cause offence to someone? If Jo were here, working on one of the stalls, he would not be walking with Fliss. Not because he never spoke to single women—he had contact with people in all walks of life. But because, in his heart, a spark of interest had been struck, and if he said it hadn't, he was lying to himself.

"I'm sorry," Fliss said. "I didn't mean to make you sad."

He looked down at her, deciding to be honest. "I was thinking about what you said last night. That loving another woman wouldn't be a betrayal and wouldn't mean loving Jo any less. I don't know if I believe that. And I don't think it's fair to enter a relationship without giving a hundred percent."

"Not everyone believes in soul mates," she said. "Or perfection. Not everyone is as idealistic as that. Me? I'd be content with a guy who was faithful and honest and loving. I wouldn't expect to be his first or only love."

"But you deserve to be adored. To be admired. To be put on a pedestal and worshipped. All women do."

Her lips curved. "You're just an old romantic."

"Maybe. What's wrong with that?"

"Nothing. It's sweet. But it's not realistic. It's setting your expectations so high that you can only fail to reach them. When girls are young, I'm sure they all dream about finding Mr. Right, that one man they're supposed to be with, who'll love them completely, and with whom they'll be happy for the rest of their lives. But I don't believe in soul mates, or in perfect love. Relationships take work. At the minimum, they need faithfulness and loyalty. And if they come with companionship and compatibility and affection, that's amazing and not to be sniffed at. Passion is great, but it fades over time, and there has to be more than that beneath it to sustain the relationship."

"I think you should be the counselor," he joked.

She shrugged. "Seems like common sense to me. You met and married a girl and you were devoted to her for many years. Any woman who expected you to love her the way you love your wife is crazy. But that doesn't mean you can't have another loving, fulfilling relationship." She stopped by a stall selling homemade chocolates. "Ooh. I'm going to have to purchase some of these."

Dominic stood back and watched her pick from the selection of truffles, which were placed carefully in a small box. A lock of hair had escaped her hat and curled around her cheek, and he watched her tuck it behind her ear.

Her words warmed him. He didn't know that he agreed with them; it still didn't seem fair to have a relationship when you knew you couldn't give your whole heart to that person. Everyone deserved to be the most important person in someone else's life, and it seemed wrong to commit to someone knowing full well that there was a corner of your heart that would remain forever unavailable to them, as if they'd moved into your house and discover a locked attic that you refused to open.

It also didn't erase the fact that he'd promised Jo he'd never love another woman.

But the words warmed him, just the same.

It saddened him too, though, that Fliss was ready to settle for less than a perfect relationship. That she considered only faithfulness and loyalty the bar by which she judged possible mates. Those things were important, of course, but she'd obviously been scarred so much that the notion of finding someone who felt that way about her but was also madly in love with her seemed impossible.

He hoped she found that man. No doubt she had many faults he hadn't yet been party to, but to his eyes she was beautiful, gentle, kind, and sexy, and she deserved a man who would give her all his heart, and who would worship the ground she walked on.

She came back over with the box of truffles and offered them to him. He picked one and bit into it, his mouth flooding with the taste of mint and chocolate.

She did the same, closing her eyes momentarily as she sighed. "Mmm, coffee. My favorite."

Dominic licked his fingers, knowing at that moment that whenever he tasted chocolate, he would think about this afternoon, about the bright autumn sunshine on his skin, the sound of children's laughter in the background, and the way Fliss's words had given him hope for the first time since his wife had died.

Chapter Eleven

When Fliss finally got back to the house, Roberta told her to have a rest while she put on the dinner. She went into her room, changed out of her clothes into a comfortable tee and track pants, and sat on the bed for a while, thinking about her day and the time she'd spent with Dominic.

Then she picked up her phone and turned it on.

For a while, she just skimmed through her emails, Facebook messages, and tweets. It looked as if Jack hadn't yet released the rest of the photos. There was a lot of speculation about them and the video, most of it unpleasant, and much talk about the fact that she'd gone dark and nobody knew where she was. Fans were begging each other to tweet if they thought they'd seen her. She scrolled through the tweets, but nobody had mentioned New Zealand yet, so she'd escaped being detected so far. Some of her loyal fans were standing up for her and saying everyone should respect her privacy, but most people were interested in what was happening between her and Jack, desperate to see how she'd react when the photos came out, and what would happen to her career. Although many of them were painting Jack as the bad guy, saying how terrible it was that a man could do this to his girlfriend, she suspected that they were secretly hoping she'd implode as that made better news than her standing up for herself. People were so cruel. Feeling nauseous, she quickly left the sites, her stomach churning.

Anger flooded her. Jack was the one who'd cheated. She'd made the decision not to announce that because, firstly, she wasn't sure that everyone would understand how betrayed she felt when he hadn't actually slept with the other woman, as far as she knew, and, secondly, she wanted to feel good about herself and not be the type of person who shared everything online to get votes. But she was beginning to have second thoughts. What right did he have to ruin her life like this?

On the night that her friend had said she'd seen him kissing another woman, Fliss had confronted him, and they'd had a huge argument. She'd screamed and cried; he'd yelled and slammed doors. Eventually, she'd walked out. Since then, she hadn't spoken to him, even when he'd released the photo. Kurt had advised her to keep her distance because she was never going to win, and she'd done as he'd suggested, even though part of her had burned to confront him.

She hadn't yet gotten around to removing Jack from her speed dial. She pressed the button, held the phone to her ear, and stood to look out of the window. It was late in LA, but she knew he'd still be up.

He answered after two rings. "Fliss. You are still alive. I was beginning to wonder if someone had kidnapped you." He sounded amused rather than concerned.

She bit her lip at the sound of his voice, fresh tears of hurt and fury stinging her eyes. But she kept her voice calm. "I needed to get away."

"Fair enough." He exhaled as if he'd sat down. Was he on his own? Or was another woman there, lying in bed, waiting for him to come back?

Now she had him on the phone, she didn't know what she wanted to say. Kurt was right, she would never win a conversation with him. She wouldn't be able to say anything to make him feel guilty for what he was doing. The guy had no soul, or else he wouldn't have posted the photo in the first place.

She could shout, scream, rail at him, but she'd done that already, and where had it gotten her? She'd heard her high-pitched voice ranting at him, had dashed frustrated tears from her eyes, and it hadn't solved anything.

"What do you want?" he said.

In the garden, Roberta emerged and bent to pick some herbs for whatever dish she was concocting. She shooed some chickens away, then stood and stretched, her hands on her hips, her face lifted to the late afternoon sun. Even though she obviously hadn't met her Mr. Right yet, and she'd talked about wanting a family, she looked happy and content in her little garden, and Fliss envied her.

It had been a mistake to call Jack. He sounded the same, his deep, husky voice still sexy, bringing memories of lying in bed, her back to his chest, him kissing her neck as he murmured the things he'd like to do to her. She'd thought he'd loved her, but it was all a lie. She'd told the truth to Dominic—she didn't believe there was one man in the world with whom she was supposed to be, and she didn't expect fireworks and the kind of love she saw in the movies. But she did believe in faithfulness and monogamy. And clearly those things meant nothing to Jack. Not like they did to Dominic, who had loved his wife so much that he felt guilty about the thought of being with another woman, even two years after she'd died. The thought made a tear roll down Fliss's cheek.

"Are you still there?" Jack said impatiently.

"I'm not going to ask you not to release the photos," she said, "because I know you will, no matter what I say. I know your five minutes of fame is important to you, and so is the money. But I'm not going to beg. And I'm not going to tell the world why we broke up to get back at you. I'm a bigger person than that, or at least, I aspire to be. I just want you to know that I loved you. And I hope that one day you'll look back on these few weeks and think about what you've done with some regret."

He was silent for a moment. Then he said, "Even if I do, at least I'll be doing it with a load of cash in my pocket."

She swallowed hard. "You know I might lose the Whitfield role because of this?"

"Yeah. What a shame." He sounded bored. "I gotta go."

Her fingers tightened into fists so tightly that her nails dug into her palms. "What did I ever do to you, Jack, to make you treat me like this?"

"Yeah, 'cause you're so fucking perfect. You're like a doll, Fliss, a Barbie doll that your mother dressed when you were young, and your agent played with when you grew up. You do what everyone tells you, and you don't have a fucking mind of your own."

She stared out the window, not seeing the garden anymore, her mind spinning. "What?"

"You don't give a fuck about Hollywood, and yet you have Whitfield sniffing around you because of *Love for a Lifetime*, which was only successful because I was in it."

"Bullshit," she said. "You were no more famous than I was when we made that movie."

"Whatever. You believe what you want. You're beautiful, Fliss, I'll give you that, but you're a fucking ice queen. Even in bed. You go through the motions with everything, but inside, you're just empty. Everyone says you have an amazing screen presence, but they don't realize it's all fake, it's just a charade. Take the mask off, and in real life there's nothing beneath it." He blew out a breath. "Gotta go," he said again, and hung up.

Fliss lowered the phone slowly. Then she turned, went over to the bed, and sat.

His words had been incredibly cruel. And yet, wasn't that exactly what she'd thought herself? That she wore a mask, and when she took it off, nobody recognized her? Maybe he was right, and her persona was all an act, and deep down she was empty, her heart a dry husk, her character a shadow of the Felicity Rivers who appeared on screen.

You're a fucking ice queen. Even in bed. That stung. It was true that she hadn't had a huge amount of experience compared to some actresses who'd been linked with every leading male they'd performed with. She'd had a few partners when she was young, at college, and she'd had a fling with one of the actors from Shortland Street. She'd then had a relationship and had lived with the lead actor in her first movie for a year. But that was it, hardly a long list. None of her partners had complained about her being cold or bad in bed. She liked sex, and she'd thought she was fairly good at it. But maybe it was all in her head. Jack had been demanding and aggressive in the bedroom, and while sometimes he'd been a bit more than she could handle, she'd done her best to please him. But clearly, she hadn't done enough.

Well, fuck him! She wasn't going to sit there and dissolve into self-pity because the guy who'd cheated on her had called her names. She was bigger than that, wasn't she? Fuck Jack and his photos and his insults.

Getting up, she tossed her phone into her suitcase and left the room, going out into the kitchen. Roberta stood at the stove, frying vegetables and meat, but she glanced over as Fliss came out. "Hey, you. Everything all right? I thought I heard you talking, but you must have been on the phone."

Fliss put her hand to her mouth and burst into tears.

"Oh, shit." Alarmed, Roberta put down her wooden spoon and came over. "Here, sit down. I'm so sorry."

"It's not your fault." Fliss sat at the table and put her face in her hands. "I'm so sorry. I don't want to cry. I'm frustrated, that's all."

Roberta passed her a piece of kitchen towel, stirred the frying meat, and came back over. "Who were you talking to?"

"Jack."

"Oh shit. Did he ring?"

"No, I called him. It was stupid; I shouldn't have done it. I'm such an idiot."

"No you're not, you had every right to call him. Fucking bastard. What did you say? Did you ask him not to post the photos?"

Fliss fought for control, wiping her eyes, but couldn't stop the tears coming. "No. I tried to take the high ground. But he dragged me down. And he was just so… cruel. I tried to stand up for myself but the things he said… I think they were true. And oh my God, that hurts." She put her face in her hands again.

Roberta sighed and walked away. Fliss heard the clink of glasses, the metallic sound of a wine bottle being unscrewed, and the glug of liquid being poured into a glass. Then she came back and put the glasses on the table. "Have a couple of mouthfuls," she said. "We're going to get drunk tonight."

Fliss wiped her face, had a big mouthful of wine, and swallowed it down. It was a Syrah, the peppery plum tones warming as it traveled down into her stomach. "Oh, that's nice."

"It's a local wine, from a friend of mine who runs a vineyard at Blue Penguin Bay. I'll take you up there at some point." Roberta had some herself, moved the frying pan off the heat, then came back to sit at the table. "What did he say, exactly?"

Fliss gave her the gist of the conversation, leaving out the bit about sex. "The terrible thing is, I think he's right," she whispered. "I know I put on this mask when I'm on screen, and I can feel myself take it off. I walked all through town today, right across the domain to the primary school, and nobody recognized me at all."

"That's because you had a hat on and sunglasses. And because they weren't looking for you."

"I don't know…"

"Look," Roberta said somewhat fiercely, "I take your word that you thought this guy was decent in the beginning, but he sounds like a fucking dickhead. And his opinion isn't worth a shit. Just because someone says something doesn't make it so. He wants to hurt you. Of *course* he does! He was dating the most beautiful actress who's about to crash into Hollywood so hard they won't know what's coming, and she dumped him and landed an amazing part almost on the same day. He's ashamed and angry and embarrassed and envious all at once, and he wants to hurt you because then it'll make him feel as if he's the one who's in the right and you deserve to be treated badly. Unless he's a complete psychopath—and I'm not ruling that out—he's got to be feeling bad beneath it all, even if he's refusing to admit it and covering it with rage."

"Maybe." Fliss blew her nose and had another mouthful of wine. "I'm not so sure."

"Well, let's not talk about him because we don't care about him. All we care about is you. And you're too good to let some little shit bring you down." Roberta stabbed the table with her finger. "You are better than that. You're not cold and empty. You're funny, and warm, and kind."

"He said I was bad in bed," Fliss said sadly.

"Well, he would say that. He's lost you. I bet his dick was the size of a peanut."

Fliss coughed into her wine, unable to hide a laugh. "Actually, he wasn't that big."

"There you go. There's no such thing as a girl being bad in bed, honey. We're as good as the men we're with. If we love someone and he takes time to show us what he enjoys, and we do the same, everything's hunky dory. What he means is that he obviously wanted you to do something kinky and you weren't keen and that means you're frigid. What fucking bullshit."

Fliss gave her a wry look. "I love you, do you know that?"

"Aw. I love you too." She reached over and gave Fliss a hug. "But I'm right, aren't I?"

"Kind of. I like sex."

"Good."

"But I'm not into everything. He liked taking risks, you know, doing it outdoors, in toilets and cupboards and stuff. I hate it when I think you're going to be discovered. I can't relax if I think someone's going to open the door at any minute."

"There you go. Fucking pervert."

Fliss coughed again. "You are wicked," she murmured.

"But I make you smile." Roberta kissed her forehead as she rose. "Okay, I'm getting dinner now, so we'll have something to soak up the wine. I have a cupboard full of amazing reds. Get your drinking hat on! Tonight, we're going to bitch about every man we've ever been with. Okay?"

"Okay," Fliss said, somewhat happily. She had lots of acquaintances, but she couldn't have done this with any of them. Thank God Roberta had invited her up here. What would she have done without her?

Her mind lingered briefly on Dominic, and the lovely afternoon they'd shared, wandering around the school fair. What a gorgeous guy. If she'd been dating him, he'd never have kissed another woman. *You deserve to be adored. To be admired. To be put on a pedestal and worshipped.*

Hmm. She could think of worse things than being worshipped by a guy like Dominic Goldsmith.

Chapter Twelve

"Is Fliss coming to the party tomorrow?" Emily asked.

Dominic glanced across at the sofa, where she was lying stretched out. It was early evening, the clouds had finally taken over the bright blue sky, and it was raining lightly. Emily had had her bath, and, because it was Saturday, she was allowed to stay up a little later and watch a movie with him. He'd poured himself a whisky, and he was sitting in the armchair with his feet propped on the coffee table.

"Uh… yeah. I think so," he said.

"Maybe you should ring to make sure," she said.

"I asked her," he replied. "And Roberta's coming. So, if Fliss wants to come, she can come with Roberta."

"Yeah, but maybe you should call just to make sure."

He narrowed his eyes at her. "What's going on?"

"Well, I told Kaia that Fliss is American but that she can also sound like a Kiwi, and Kaia's coming tomorrow, and she wants to meet Fliss for herself and see if I'm right."

She was right—Fliss had put on a Kiwi accent at the fair, presumably so as not to draw attention to herself. Dominic was surprised his daughter had noticed it. "I don't think Fliss wants to be gawped at like a tiger in a cage at the zoo."

"That's not what I meant." She sat up, crossing her legs. "Aw, come on, Dad. Ring her and make sure she's coming, then I can call Kaia."

He looked at his phone, sitting on the coffee table. "I don't have her number."

"Ring Roberta."

"She's probably busy."

"Dad…"

He huffed a sigh, paused the movie, and picked up the phone. "All right, stop nagging." But it was good-natured, because deep down he wanted to talk to Fliss again. When she'd turned up at his stall, it had been like the sun had come out.

He pressed the button to dial Roberta's number and put the phone to his ear.

It rang for so long he thought it was going to go to her message, but finally she answered. "Hell….oooo?"

He frowned. "Roberta?"

"Dominic! We were just talking about you."

"Oh? Good things, I hope."

"Fliss wants to know whether you wear boxers or briefs."

"Roberta!" Fliss's horrified voice echoed in the background, and Roberta giggled.

Dominic's lips curved up. "Are you two drunk?"

"No! Not at all. Not one bit. Okay, maybe a little bit. She needed some consolification. I mean consolidation. What do I mean?"

"Consolation?" he asked, laughing.

"Yes! That's it."

"Can I talk to her?"

"Hold on." He heard her talking to Fliss, their voices muffled. Then she came back. "She's too embarrassed."

"For Christ's sake… Rob, put her on."

There was a scrabbling noise, and then Fliss said hesitantly, "Hello?"

"Hey." He didn't miss the leap his heart gave. "How are you?"

She sighed. "I rang Jack."

His smile faded. "Oh." He got to his feet and wandered over to the window. The garden was overgrown, and the lawn needed mowing.

"I don't know why I did," she said softly. "After seeing you, I felt positive for the first time in ages, and I suppose I thought maybe I'd be able to have a sensible discussion with him."

"You don't have to explain yourself to me."

She continued as if he hadn't spoken. "But as soon as I spoke to him, I knew I'd made a mistake. I would never have been able to convince him that what he's doing is wrong."

"Did you try?"

"I told him that I hope he'll look back on these weeks one day and feel regret."

"What did he say?"

"He said 'even if I do, at least I'll be doing it with a load of cash in my pocket.'"

Dominic felt an uncharacteristic surge of anger. "I'm so sorry."

"It's okay," she said, in a voice that said it was very far from okay.

"Tell him the rest of it," Roberta said in the background.

"I don't want to."

There was a muffled conversation, and then Roberta came back onto the phone.

"Fucking bastard," she said.

"Yeah," Dominic replied. "I agree."

"He called her an ice queen and said there was nothing beneath the mask she wore when she acted, and that she was bad in bed. I want to smash the fucker's face in."

Dominic was genuinely bemused that a man could be so cruel to a woman he'd shared himself with. "Me too. So does Emily." He glanced over his shoulder, winking at Emily as he saw her raised eyebrows.

Roberta gave a short laugh. "She's pretty upset about it, but we're drowning our sorrows in Blue Penguin Bay's 2016 Syrah."

"Fair enough. Can I talk to her again?"

"Hold on."

More rustling.

"Hello," Fliss said softly.

"Emily wants to know if you're coming to the party tomorrow," Dominic said. "She wants to show her friend how you can speak both Kiwi and American."

"Aw." He could almost hear the smile in her voice. "That's sweet."

"Can I tell her you'll be there?"

"Of course. I'll see you then."

"Sleep well," he said, "and don't try to keep up with Roberta; she could drink a sailor under the table."

She laughed. "Okay."

"Oh, and Fliss?"

"Hmm?"

"Boxer-briefs," he said. "The tight sort. Usually black."

"Oh my God. Just kill me now."

He chuckled and hung up. Turning, he saw Emily's stare and laughed. "Don't ask."

She patted the sofa, and he sat next to her. "She's nice," Emily said.

"She is."

"Why are they getting drunk?"

"It helps grownups when they get stressed sometimes."

"Why is Fliss stressed?"

He sighed and leaned back, his arm along the top of the sofa, and Emily curled up against him. His method of parenting, especially since Jo had died, had been to be as honest as he could with his daughter. "I'll tell you a bit," he said, "but you mustn't tell anyone, not even Kaia, okay?"

"Okay, Daddy."

"She's had some trouble back in America. She had a boyfriend, and her friend saw him kissing another woman."

"Oh."

"He said that wasn't wrong, but Fliss thinks it was, and it hurt her feelings, so she broke up with him. And then he took a photo he had of her and posted it on the internet."

"That wasn't very nice."

"It wasn't. He has more photos, and he's trying to sell them."

"Sell them?"

"Well, Fliss is a little bit famous. She's a Hollywood actress."

Emily thought about that. "What sort of photos are they?"

"I don't know; I haven't seen the one he's posted. The point is that they were private, and he made them public against her wishes."

"She must be very angry."

"She is. And she's hurt. She loved this man, and he's been very unpleasant to her." He kissed the top of his daughter's head.

Emily was quiet for a moment, and he knew she was thinking about what he'd told her. Sure enough, eventually she said, "Do you think her boyfriend kissing another woman was wrong?"

"I do."

"If he said it was just a kiss, why was she so upset?"

"Kisses aren't something you should give away lightly. They're to be shared with someone special. When you agree to be with a person, you shouldn't share yourself with anyone else."

"But they weren't married."

"It doesn't matter. You should be faithful in any relationship. Marriage is just the final promise that you'll love that person forever."

"Not forever."

"Until you die, that's pretty much forever."

"Until they die. That's different."

He lifted his arm from her shoulders and moved forward. "I'm not going to argue with you about this again."

Her face crumpled. "I'm sorry."

"You can't keep telling me that what I feel is wrong, Emily. It's not fair. One day, you'll meet a man who will be your whole world. Until then, you're not in a position to comment on how it feels to lose someone."

A tear ran down her cheek.

He closed his eyes for a moment, then leaned back and hugged her. "I'm sorry. Please don't cry. I miss Mum, that's all. I still feel married to her, and that means that thinking about dating someone else feels wrong. Can you understand that?"

She nodded, burying her face in his arm. "I just want you to be happy, Daddy."

"I am happy, sweetheart. I have you."

"But one day I'll have to leave, and then you'll be alone."

He swallowed hard. She'd always been older than her years, but it surprised him that at nearly eight she'd given thought to the day that she would leave home, whether it was for university or some other path. And not just that she'd be going, but that she'd be leaving him behind. The fact that this might be the driving force behind her pushing him to date again shocked him. It also made him feel extremely humble to think that his own daughter had such a large heart that she could think further than her own needs and desires.

"You shouldn't worry about that," he scolded, tightening his arm around her. "My job keeps me busy, and even when you do go to university, you'll be coming home a lot."

"But everyone should have someone of their own," she whispered. "It's not fair that just because you were married once, you can't ever marry again."

"It's not that I can't… I don't want to."

"Well, I don't ever want to get married if it means I can't love anyone else ever," she said fiercely. "It's not your fault that Mum died. She left us."

He frowned. "It wasn't her choice, honey."

"Then I hate God for taking her away."

Dominic leaned his head on the back of the sofa. It wasn't the first time they'd had this conversation. He knew that his daughter was still struggling to deal with the death of her mother, trying to understand why Jo had been taken at such a relatively young age, when at school other kids' mothers came to their sports day and their school plays. But it was hard to know what to say when she got to the stage of blaming God.

He blew out a breath. He needed another whisky.

"I didn't mean that," she said, her voice muffled in his shirt.

"I think it's time for bed," he told her gently.

"But we haven't finished the movie."

"We'll finish it tomorrow. Go on, brush your teeth and get in, then you can read your book to me."

He turned off the TV, went into Emily's room and listened to her read one of her school books for a while, then read her a chapter of *Watership Down*. She found some of the words a struggle, but she loved listening to the stories about the rabbits.

They said a short prayer together, then he kissed her goodnight and went out and closed the door.

Going into the living room, he poured himself a small second whisky, and, leaving the light off, sat in his chair, and looked out into the dark garden.

Jo had put solar lights all around the fence a few years ago. One line of them flashed weakly; the other had stopped working a while back. He really needed to take them down and buy new ones. Actually, the whole garden needed a complete overhaul. Her roses had died, and the flowerbeds were overgrown. He'd left everything for too long, thinking that time would somehow preserve it, but of course time marched on, and the world continued to revolve, unmindful of the momentous changes that had happened in his life.

He thought about his father for a while, missing him too. Hugh Goldsmith had been solid and supportive, never judgmental. Pursing his lips, Dominic leaned over, grabbed his phone, and dialed his mother's number.

"Hello?" she answered, sounding surprised.

"It's me," he said.

"Hey, you. Everything all right?" she asked, as he rarely rang in the evening.

"I was thinking about Dad."

"Aw," she said. "Me too."

He had a mouthful of whisky and slid down in the armchair so he could rest his head on the back. "Do you think you'll ever get married again?"

She gave a soft laugh. "I very much doubt it. I can't imagine dating again—the thought horrifies me."

"I know what you mean."

"And as for… anything else, the sheer thought of taking my clothes off in front of a stranger gives me hives."

He chuckled. "You're not old."

"I'm fifty-two. Even my wrinkles have wrinkles."

"Any man would be lucky to have you," he said.

"Come on, Dom, we're in the same boat, aren't we? We've both had a happy marriage. We both know how unlikely it would be to find that again." She paused for a moment, then said, "Unless… Have you met someone?"

He thought of Fliss and had another, large swallow of whisky. "No."

"Is she American, by any chance?"

He blew out a breath. "That's not why I'm ringing. I mean… maybe she's sparked off something. An awareness, I suppose. Emily was talking tonight about what will happen when she goes off to university and leaves me all alone."

"Oh, what a sweetheart. She's not against you meeting someone else, then?"

"Quite the opposite. She wants to be a bridesmaid at my wedding."

Noelle laughed. "I can imagine. That dress she wore to Phoebe's wedding could almost walk on its own by the time you got it off her."

"She even wore it to bed."

She chuckled. "Has she given you food for thought, though?"

"Yes. No. I don't know. I suppose I wanted to ask you… If you were to meet someone, do you think you'd feel unfaithful to Dad?"

"I'm not sure. Maybe, initially. We never had that conversation that people talk about, you know, 'if I die and you meet someone else I'll haunt you,' or something like that. Did you and Jo?"

"No. But it's on my mind."

"That she might haunt you?"

"Well, strictly speaking, we don't believe in ghosts in the Church."

"Oh, hmm, right."

"Being haunted by our own memories is something else, though. Plus, I can't overlook the fact that I'm supposed to set an example to the community. I can't just go off having affairs with every woman I take a fancy to."

"More's the pity."

"Mum…"

"Oh sweetheart, you were never this serious when you were young."

"Yeah, I know, but I grew up. And I fell in love. And I promised to love her forever, not just in the eyes of the law, but in the eyes of God. And then I lost her. Now what do I do?" He fell silent and closed his eyes.

"You follow your heart," she said softly. "You're not a saint, sweetheart. You're just a man. A very good man, but a man nevertheless. And you need physical and emotional comfort and companionship. Does that mean you should sleep around and flaunt it in front of your parishioners? Of course not. But if you meet someone who warms you right through and who's prepared to offer you comfort, should you turn her down? I don't know, that's a question only you can answer. Personally, I don't think that love can be bad, no matter in what form it arrives. I don't think you can be unfaithful to someone who's passed away." Her voice turned husky. "I loved your father terribly—still do—but if I had the chance to love and be loved by another man, I don't know that I'd be strong enough to walk away from that. It wouldn't mean I'd love your dad any less. Just that I'm only human and being on your own can get lonely."

"You don't think I should have higher standards, though? Because of my position?"

"I don't believe in my heart that God would think badly of you for finding comfort with someone two years after your wife died. You've mourned, sweetheart. You're a good boy. Strong, kind, sensible. Don't you think you deserve a bit of fun?"

He stared into his glass.

"I'd better go," she said. "Think about it, eh?"

"Sure. Sleep well."

"You too. Goodnight, honey." She hung up.

Dominic tossed his phone onto the sofa, then sat there sipping his whisky, looking out into the night.

Chapter Thirteen

Roberta pulled off the state highway onto a short drive that curved in front of a long, low house, slotted the car amongst the others at the end of the drive, and turned off the car engine.

Fliss got out and looked around her in delight. Huge palm trees and curling silver ferns lined the drive. There was a front lawn circled by carefully tended flower borders, and at the back she could just see an enormous lawn with a pond and a palm island in the middle. The land was surrounded by tall evergreens that gave the place a secluded feel. The jasmine by the front door lent the air a fragrant, rich smell, making the warm afternoon feel summery, even though it was technically autumn.

"Nice day for it," Roberta said.

"It's a beautiful day." Fliss had forgotten how delightful the weather was in the Northland. She'd assumed her memories of long, hot, humid summers were childhood selectiveness, but it appeared they were more accurate that she'd thought.

Alone with the smell of jasmine, the aroma of barbecued food floated on the breeze, together with the sound of laughter and the strumming of a guitar.

"Well, we know Dom's here," Roberta said, gesturing with her head for Fliss to follow her.

Boxer-briefs. The tight sort. Usually black. Fliss's lips curved up as she followed Roberta around the front of the house and down the side to the deck that ran the length of the house. She felt a flutter of nerves in her stomach but put it down to being in a strange setting, and fear of someone recognizing her.

As she turned the corner, though, and her gaze fell immediately on Dominic sitting in the middle of the group of people, playing his guitar, she knew she was fooling herself.

He saw her first, and he put down his guitar and rose with a smile as she and Roberta approached. Everyone else turned, and there was a flurry of movement and sound as some people rose to greet them, and others called out hello.

Fliss shook hands and accepted a few kisses on the cheek. Bianca and her twin sister, Phoebe, were there, and she met Phoebe's new husband, Rafe, a good-looking guy who could have played the lead role in any romcom movie. She met Elliot, a slightly shorter, slenderer, more mischievous form of his older brother, and Elliot's girlfriend, Karen, short, dark, and girl-next-door pretty. Noelle was there, of course, as it was her house, and another guy that Roberta introduced as "Dr. Angus," which made him roll his eyes and say, "Just call me Angus." The last couple were Libby, who helped Roberta out in the shop, and Mike, her partner, another cop, a stocky guy who appeared to have no sense of humor judging by the way he sat back and hardly smiled, even though the others were joking and teasing.

Fliss wasn't sure if everyone present knew who she was, but nobody commented on her movies or said anything about her predicament or the photo, and for that she was grateful.

Dominic waited for her to finish meeting everyone, then smiled as she turned to him.

"Hello," he said.

"Hey." She brushed a strand of hair from her face.

"What can I get you to drink?" he asked.

"Um, a soda please. Diet Coke? Something like that?"

He grinned and led her over to the table on the deck that held all the bottles of wine and drink. "How's the head?" he asked, scooping some ice from a bucket into a tall glass, popping the top on a can, and pouring the soda over the ice.

"Not too bad." She gave him a wry look. "I haven't drunk that much in a long time." Taking the glass from him, she glanced at his T-shirt, and her lips curved up. "I'm quite glad you're not wearing your collar. I'd have to do some kind of penance."

He poured himself a Coke. "You do realize that when I take the collar off, I'm still the same person under it?"

She laughed. "I guess."

"A bit like you," he said, sipping the Coke, keeping his gaze on her. He was referring to Jack's comment from last night.

She met his gaze, then dropped hers. "I wish I hadn't told you about that."

He led her a little away from the others along the deck, then stopped and leaned a shoulder against a post. "Why?"

She shrugged, turning the glass in her hands. "It makes me feel... dirty." Her lips twisted. "And not in a good way."

He didn't smile. His green eyes surveyed her, their directness sending a little shiver down her back. "That man has no power over you," he said, his tone firm. "Only what you choose to give him. What he's doing is wrong, Fliss. Not just releasing the photos, but saying such cruel, untrue things to you."

She studied her shoes. "I don't know that they are untrue."

"Bullshit."

She raised her gaze, amused. "I'm guessing that's the man and not the deacon talking?"

"I'm just a man, as my mother keeps trying to tell me. It's obvious bullshit. Calling you cold? You're *hot as*." He blinked. "Actually, that came out wrong."

She laughed, her face warming. "That's a lovely thing to say, thank you. I know I'm very lucky that I don't look like the back end of a bus. But it doesn't matter how pretty a person's face is if she's empty inside."

"You're not empty inside," he said huskily, "that's what I was trying to say in my very clumsy way. I can read people—I have to, it's part of my job. I've met people who are empty inside—on drugs, or so beaten by the world that they have nothing left to give. You're so far removed from that I can't tell you. I can see inside you, Fliss, and I know you have a good heart. You're warm and funny; you make me laugh. You're the first person I've thought of when I've opened my eyes the last few days and the last one in my head before I've gone to sleep. That's got to mean something."

His words were so unexpected that she stared at him, open-mouthed, touched, shocked, and flattered beyond belief.

"Fliss!"

She blinked and turned to see Emily with a slender Maori girl at her side. "Hello," Fliss said, forcing a smile on her face.

"This is my friend, Kaia." Emily pushed the blushing girl forward.

"Hello, Kaia," Fliss said. "I hear you're interested in accents."

Kaia's blush deepened. "I just don't know how you can switch from one to the other."

"It's easy. For instance, now I sound American, right? My vowels are *looong*. But Kiwis say some of the vowels differently. Like... I want an egg and a pen and a pin." She changed her accent, so it sounded like *I want an igg and a pin and a pn*.

Kaia and Emily laughed and clapped their hands. "I told you," Emily said with delight.

Dominic grinned and ushered the girls away, telling them to go and play with the Swingball in the center of the lawn, and they rushed off, talking and giggling all the while.

"Oh to be eight again," Fliss sighed, following him down the steps onto the grass and over to the barbecue, where the men were attempting to cremate all the meat.

"I wouldn't be that age again if you paid me," Dominic said, peering over Elliot's shoulder where he was poking the sausages. "Don't keep turning them. They won't brown."

"You wanna fucking do it?" Elliot offered him the tongs.

"The apron suits you much better."

Elliot ignored him and started flipping the burgers.

"Looks great," Dominic said, "if you like charcoal with your meat."

Elliot gave him the finger, and they bickered good-naturedly. Fliss smiled, seeing in them the teenage brothers they'd once been, arguing over rugby or girls.

"They've never been any different," Noelle said, coming up with a couple of plates on which they could place the cooked meat. "Men are just boys with slightly more expensive toys."

The two of them watched Rafe attempting to juggle with the tongs and two spoons, while Angus stole a sausage from the corner when he thought nobody was looking.

"I can see what you mean," Fliss said.

Noelle smiled. "How are you doing?"

"I'm okay, thanks." Fliss wasn't sure how much Noelle knew about her background and decided not to fill her in. "It's a lovely day for a barbecue."

"We're heading into winter now, and it'll start growing cooler and rainier, so we might as well make the most of the nice weather." Noelle gave the guys the plates. "How are we doing?"

"Ready to go." Elliot started plating the burgers while Dominic poked the sausages.

"I'll help dish up," Fliss said, going over to the table where the food would be laid.

She and Roberta had brought a couple of salads with them that they'd made earlier—one a pasta in an amazing cherry sauce that Roberta had conjured up, and another an Israeli couscous salad with chopped cooked vegetables. She took the plastic wrap off the bowls, her mouth watering at the sight of the other dishes: a potato salad with chopped bacon, a fresh tomato salsa, bowls of crisp lettuce with sliced onion, cucumber, and tomato, and various rolls and buns to put the sausages and burgers in. Elliot had also grilled some vegetable kebabs and some prawn kebabs, and she peeled the foil off those plates.

As Dominic brought over the sausages, everyone came up to help themselves. Fliss dished herself up a small dinner and took it back to the group of chairs, choosing a seat next to Roberta, and the seats were gradually filled as people returned with their plates of food to eat.

They ate and talked and laughed and ate some more, and Fliss finished everything on her plate and also managed to find space for some of Libby's fruit salad with a splash of cream. When she'd done, she felt stuffed full and pleasantly content. How nice to be able to eat whatever she wanted without her mother or the diners in a restaurant or other actors or even her own inner judgment watching, ready to criticize.

"Oh, that was lovely," she said, stretching out her legs and thanking Emily as she collected her empty plate and took it inside for her grandmother.

"Come on, Dom." Bianca lay down on the swing seat when Roberta rose to fetch a drink. "Play something for us."

"All right." He lifted his guitar onto his lap and picked out a few notes. "What do you want to hear?"

"Something to suit a warm Sunday evening."

He started strumming, beginning with Elvis's *Fever*, sending tingles all down Fliss's back. His previous words to her circled around her head like tweety birds on a cartoon movie. *You're the first person I've thought of when I've opened my eyes the last few days and the last one in my head before I've gone to sleep. That's got to mean something.*

It was pointless to know that because she was going back to the States soon, so nothing could happen here. And besides, she had enough on her plate, and had no interest in having a fling with a preacher.

Okay, maybe she had a little interest.

She let her gaze linger on him as he moved on to another song. He was listening to Elliot and Angus talking about rugby, his fingers moving across the strings automatically, his gaze flicking over to them every now and then. He was relaxed and comfortable in his own skin, and she liked that. She liked his no-nonsense approach to life, and although she wasn't religious herself, she admired his faith and his attitude to people and life in general.

He was also *sexy as*. She smiled at the Kiwi-ism.

He looked over at her at that moment and caught her smile. His own lips curved up in response, and he winked at her.

Fliss blushed like a fourteen-year-old and looked out across the garden, her face burning. Well, that was weird. She hadn't blushed so badly in years. Maybe it was the menopause hitting early. Very early.

The evening wore on, the food gradually disappearing and drinks flowing along with the laughter. When Dominic finally declared he needed a break, Noelle put some music on, as it was clear that nobody looked ready to go.

Fliss eventually gave in and had a glass of wine, feeling so far removed from her life in America that it was as if she was another person. Maybe she should just leave it all behind. The movies and the parties and the people that deep down she really disliked, because they were so shallow and cared for nothing but how they looked and how other people perceived them.

Her gaze drifted back to Dominic, as it had many times that evening. He'd kept his distance, but they'd exchanged glances several times, and now, when she met his eyes again, she felt a frisson of pleasure pass through her. He liked her, it was obvious by his looks and his words. Of *course* it couldn't come to anything, but that didn't mean she couldn't enjoy his company. They were both adults, not lovestruck teenagers. He'd lost his wife, and she knew he was finding it difficult coming to terms with the notion of being with someone else. So maybe talking to her helped him. That, if nothing else, was a reason not to turn away.

So when, ten minutes or so later, she rose to pour herself another glass of wine from the drinks table and he appeared beside her and said, "Fancy going for a little walk?" Fliss didn't have to think about her answer.

Chapter Fourteen

The path led away from the house, around the large pool, and down across the lawn toward the river. Dominic kept his pace slow, and Fliss seemed content to meander with him, enjoying the peace and quiet of the evening. A couple of late cicadas chirruped in the trees, and as the path trailed down to the water, the sound of the river tumbling over the rocks filled the air.

"This is the Kerikeri River," he said. "It's the same one that forms Rainbow Falls farther downstream."

Her eyebrows rose. "Oh, I didn't realize that."

"It's caused some problems in the past. In 2007, there was a great storm. Fallen tree trunks got caught on the bridge by the Stone Store and the whole basin flooded. The water stopped an inch short of the steps to the Store."

"Oh my God, really?"

"After that, they made the bypass over the river, so you can no longer drive past the Stone Store. Anyway, a few years later, there was another bad storm. The bridge upstream from here was blocked, and the whole of Mum's garden flooded." He gestured toward the pond. "You couldn't see that. The water covered the whole lawn and flooded the pool. It was a nightmare. But they've widened the banks now, so it shouldn't happen again."

"That must have been scary."

He held a branch out of the way so it didn't tangle her hair. "Mum was terrified the river wasn't going to stop rising, but the house is built on the highest point, and luckily it stopped just short of the door."

"Thank you," she said as he lowered the branch back down carefully. Her bright turquoise eyes met his for a moment, then dropped back to the path.

They walked in silence for a while, following the river, descending into the twilight of the forest. Dominic wasn't sure why he'd asked her to go for a walk. He'd done his best to keep his distance during the afternoon, but her gaze had rested on him several times, and he'd felt an answering pull in his solar plexus, as if they were linked by an invisible rope and she'd given it a tug. In the end, he'd just wanted to get her on her own, away from the others.

"You have a nice family," she said eventually.

"Yeah, they're okay. Apart from Elliot." He smiled, letting her know he didn't mean it.

"Are he and Karen married?" she asked.

"Not yet."

"You think they will be?"

He shrugged. "Not sure. She's keen, I think. Him… I don't know. Elliot keeps his cards close to his chest. He's never seemed wildly in love with her. They sort of fell into dating together and fell into getting a house together, and I expect they'll fall into getting married eventually. He buries his head in the sand—he once told me he'd let future Elliot worry about it. At the moment, he's content, and that's all he's concerned about."

"You disapprove," she said, her tone teasing.

"Eh. That makes me sound old."

"No, it makes you sound as if you set high standards for both yourself and others, and I don't see what's wrong with that. We set the bar very low in today's society, and then wonder why the divorce rate is so high."

"I think relationships take a lot more work than most are willing to give," he said. "In general, people are, at root, selfish. We all love to be loved, to be admired, to be the most important person in someone else's life, but the truth is that people aren't always willing to compromise to make it work."

He stopped by a bench that his father had placed in a small nook above the river. Colored solar lights hung in the trees nearby, casting the glade in jeweled light.

Without asking, Fliss sat on the bench, and Dominic sat next to her.

"I think you're right," she said. "And maybe that will make me take a closer look at myself in my next relationship. It's easy to think 'why isn't he paying me more attention' and forget that he's had a hard day and he's also sitting there wishing you'd massage his feet and get him a whisky."

Dominic's lips curved up. "Sounds pretty good."

She laughed, looking down at her sandals. She wore a pair of chocolate-brown wide-leg pants and a pretty cream blouse, with elegant strappy sandals. Clearly, she had money, but he had the feeling she would look beautiful and elegant even if she were dressed in a sack.

She looked up at him, then. "So... do you think you'll ever marry again?"

He watched the river, running dark and green into the trees. "A week ago, I would have said no."

"What changed?"

He turned his gaze to her and saw that it was an innocent question, although maybe a hint of hope flickered in her eyes. "Meeting you," he said.

She sucked her bottom lip and looked back at the river.

He brushed at a leaf that had fallen onto his jeans. "Some of the things you said rang true with me. About loving someone else not meaning that I'd love Jo any less."

She nodded. "I don't think we have, like, a pound of love that has to be divided between everyone we meet—four ounces to your daughter, two to your mum, that sort of thing. And if someone new comes along, I don't think you have to take from one person to give to another. I think human beings have the capacity for an endless amount of love, and it takes many forms, too. Love for children, parents, siblings. We can even love romantically in different ways. There are no rules. Only what we make for ourselves, and they're not set in stone."

"You're very wise," he said softly.

"I'm not. I'm incredibly naive."

"I don't know that the two are mutually exclusive. I think you understand the human soul, and that means you are a very trusting person. Which of course leaves you open to being manipulated."

"You think I need to stop trusting?"

"No. I don't think you should change at all."

She gave a small laugh, flicking her gaze up to his again. "You're quite a smooth talker for a preacher."

"Ha! I don't tend to think of myself as a preacher. I rarely give sermons. And certainly not with my friends! Anyway, religious men can be sexy."

"The tight black boxer-briefs do imply a certain level of sensuality."

He laughed, liking her subtle flirting. "Maybe."

"So… were you telling the truth when you said you don't have to do it in the missionary position?"

She held his gaze. Dominic's heartbeat sped up a little. He felt as if he could drown in those turquoise eyes. And the thought of Fliss being naked beneath him, or top of him, or in any position, for that matter, sent the blood shooting through his veins.

He dropped his gaze to her mouth. "Want to find out?"

He surprised himself. He hadn't planned to say the words, and once they were out, there was no going back. What a dumb thing to say. She had enough on her plate; the last thing she needed was a Church deacon still suffering from the loss of his wife coming on to her.

But she didn't jump to her feet and declare her outrage, nor did she look particularly surprised.

"Maybe," she said.

They sat there for a moment, studying each other, letting the idea settle in.

Was he really considering this? Having a… what would he call it? Affair? Fling? With a Hollywood actress? He couldn't imagine that going down very well with his congregation.

Not that they ever had to know.

Then immediately he felt guilty about even considering lying to those he cared for.

But was an omission of the truth actually a lie?

Even if the answer was no, that still meant he would finally have given up on his promise to Jo. That made him weak. It belittled his love for her. Or did it?

Fliss's expression softened, as if she could sense the way his mind was spinning. "Are deacons allowed to have sex outside marriage?" she asked.

He ran a hand through his hair. "I'm sure the technical answer is no."

"Let's put it another way. If a sixth-former—over eighteen years old—came to you, and he was young and single, and he was thinking about having a short-term fling with another sixth-former, who was also single, would you tell him to walk away?"

His lips curved up. "I'd tell him to make sure he used condoms."

She laughed. "But your religious views wouldn't affect your advice?"

"I try not to let my faith influence my role as counselor at the school, because the board doesn't want that."

"So let's change the question, then. If a parishioner came to you, and he was young and single, and he asked you the same question, what would you say?"

She tipped her head to the side, interested in his answer. He liked that she hadn't dismissed his doubts, and that she wanted to discuss this before just leaping into bed.

"I would say," he replied slowly, "that providing both parties were consenting adults, and nobody was being hurt in the process, that there is nothing wrong with sharing yourself with another person. In essence, anyway. I'm not a fan of promiscuity for the sake of sensual pleasure."

"You don't like sensual pleasure?"

"You know how to ask the hard questions, don't you? I'm a big fan of sensual pleasure. But I don't agree in using other people to get it."

"You prefer to do it yourself?" She was teasing him again. "Or is that also a no-no in the Church?"

He laughed. "'It's better to marry than to burn with passion.'"

"Is that in the Bible?"

"1 Corinthians 7:9."

"Chapter and verse."

"Damn straight."

"Is the word marry meant literally?"

He sighed. "It would have been two thousand years ago. I've always taken it more to mean that we shouldn't give in to lust for the sake of it, but that genuine sexual desire isn't dirty or sinful. Sharing yourself with someone else isn't sinful. Only if we let desire get in the way of treating someone right." He sighed again. "Or maybe I'm just interpreting what I want to hear."

"Do you think there is a form of love that is wrong?"

"Hmm. No. Only when it becomes controlling, and then it isn't love really anyway, because true love involves sacrifice and caring for other people."

"Do you think your parishioners would resent you finding love again?"

"No," he said, reluctantly, but honestly. Then he remembered old Mrs Haggett's disapproving face at the fair. "I don't know what they'd think of me having a fling, though."

He waited for her to say *Don't tell them then*, but she didn't.

She looked at the river for a while. He listened to the tumble of the water and the rustle of small animals in the undergrowth and let his thoughts and emotions run at their own pace.

He wasn't looking for justification from her. He didn't need her permission, or for her to talk him into it. But he was interested in what she had to say.

"You advised me," she said eventually, turning on the seat to face him, "about the importance of intention. If you were to have a fling with someone, and you were then asked to explain it to someone you know, maybe the question is…. how you would describe it? If it's all physical, about lust and desire and you would feel ashamed telling someone else, the answer is right there. But if it was about being lonely, and wanting comfort, and sharing yourself because you haven't done that for a long time… even if physical desire did play a part in it… would that make you feel ashamed?"

Warmth spread through him. "You are wise," he whispered. "Beyond your years."

"I just say what's in my heart."

"I can't think of a better way to be."

They were only inches apart, and his skin was prickling with the nearness of her. It had been so long since he'd had a woman in his arms. He ached to hold her, to feel her soft and warm against him. To feel her lips part, her tongue slide against his.

"I don't want to seduce you," she murmured. "I know you have doubts because you lost your wife, and you have your faith to worry about. But I like you, Dominic. I like you as a person—you're warm and kind and I trust you, which is obviously a big thing for me at the moment. But… it's not just that."

Her eyelids lowered to half-mast as her gaze dropped to his mouth. "I know it's stupid at the moment to even think about having a fling. We've both got too much going on. But from the first moment I saw you… I wanted you. Is that a terrible thing to admit?"

"It's not terrible at all," he said. "And I'm immensely flattered."

"But…" She smiled.

"But nothing. You're a beautiful, kind, clever woman who's vulnerable right now, and I don't want to take advantage of that."

She frowned. "If you mean am I looking for comfort after what's happened, yes, I suppose I am. I'm not expecting true love and a ring on my finger." She reached up a hand and cupped his face, her thumb brushing his cheek. "I thought maybe we could bring comfort to one another."

The solar lights twinkled, bringing a glow to the gathering gloom of the woods, casting shining patterns on the river's surface. Dominic felt caught up in the moment, as if he was leaning over the edge of a huge abyss. If he let go, he would plummet into its depths, and yet he couldn't know what lay at the bottom.

If he kissed her, even if he never slept with her or another woman, he'd live the rest of his life knowing he'd broken his promise to Jo, because Fliss was right, it was about intention, and if he kissed her, he would do so fully knowing and accepting what it might lead to.

But then, if it was about intention, wasn't he already damned? Hadn't he already looked at a woman other than his wife and felt desire?

He glanced away, into the woods, and held his breath. "Look." He pointed, and Fliss followed his finger.

"What?"

"There, in the leaves. It's a kiwi bird."

She stared hard, narrowing her eyes, then gasped, pressing her fingers to her mouth. The kiwi bird, big as a rabbit, the same color as the undergrowth, was barely visible, but it was there, a beautiful glimpse of a secret phenomenon so few people got to see. The bird shuffled about in the leaves, then seemed to glance at them briefly before it turned and disappeared into the bush. If he'd been looking the other way, he would never have seen it. Opportunities like that didn't come around very often.

Turning back to Fliss, he discovered her turquoise gaze studying him, waiting for him to make his decision. This gorgeous girl was offering herself to him, wanting comfort, and suddenly there was no question in his mind what he wanted to do.

Chapter Fifteen

Fliss saw the moment that Dominic decided he was going to kiss her in his eyes, and her heart leapt as he blinked, focused on her, and then his lips curved up in a small smile.

She was still cupping his face, and she held her breath as he rested an arm on the back of the seat, almost—but not quite—touching her, then moved a little closer.

He bent his head until his lips were only an inch from hers. She lifted her face, but didn't move to meet him, wanting him to take that final step himself. And he did, his breath escaping his lips to whisper across hers in a tiny sigh before he closed the distance and kissed her.

Fliss closed her eyes, sliding her hand into his hair and shifting the focus onto her other senses. Around her, she could hear the rustle of leaves, the movement of water over the rocks, the sound of music from the house way off in the distance. She could smell Dominic's aftershave, a woody fragrance with cedar and vetiver that complemented the smell of the forest around them, deep and rich.

But mostly, she concentrated on touch—on the feel of his short hair beneath her fingers, the press of his lips against hers. He was so gentle, and yet as they continued to kiss, she felt his arm come around her, his hand flat between her shoulder blades, somewhat commanding, telling her he wasn't ready to let her go.

Luckily, she wasn't ready either. She shifted on the bench, closer to him. Tilting her head, she opened her mouth, and he took the hint and slid his tongue against hers, sending her heart racing and the blood shooting around her body.

Mmm, this guy could kiss. Part of her had wondered whether a Church deacon—even one as gorgeous as Dominic—would be too self-conscious to give in to his desire. But he didn't appear to fall into that mold. Heat flowed between them, and any reservations fell away as she forgot he was a deacon, about his wife, about Jack, about everything except that here was a real man, hot and sexy, who clearly wanted her, and for a brief while she lost herself in kissing him, just enjoying being close to him.

Then, gradually, like swimming to the surface of a deep lake, she came back to herself as he lifted his head to look at her.

"Wow," she said, and pressed her lips together. "That wasn't very holy."

He chuckled and kissed her nose. "You're leading me astray."

"Corrupting you, am I?"

"Hmm. Oh well. The deed is done now."

She looked into his eyes, stroking his cheek. He meant that he'd broken his vow to his wife. He'd been unfaithful, even if it was only with a kiss. "How do you feel?"

He glanced briefly across the river, maybe searching for the kiwi, or perhaps just thinking about what they'd done. Was he regretting it?

His gaze came back to her, and to her surprise his lips quirked up. "Honestly? Horny."

She burst out laughing, tempted to reach down and check, but decided against it. She didn't want to shock him. "I guess that's a good thing."

His eyelids lowered to half-mast as he looked at her mouth. "I suppose it's to be expected. I haven't kissed a woman in a long time."

"Then I'm honored." She reached up and pressed her lips to his again, and they exchanged another long, sensual kiss.

"Thank you," she said eventually when she pulled back. "You've made my day." She touched her fingers to his lips. "I hope you don't regret it later."

"The world keeps turning," he said. "You can't stop it, no matter how hard you try. I was thinking earlier that I'd let the garden go, half thinking it would stay the way it was when Jo used to look after it. But of course, it's all overgrown now. We feel as if our world has ended, but around us plants keep growing, the sun rises and sets, and the seasons change."

It applied to them both, she thought, because when Jack had released that photo, it had felt like such a momentous event and it had brought her world crashing down around her ears. And yet everyone else had continued with their lives as if nothing had happened.

"Is there a way I can see you?" she asked. "Obviously, it's difficult for you, with Emily."

He ran a hand through his hair. "I suppose tomorrow when I drop her off with Roberta after work, I could bring you back with me. I would have to do a few house calls, but I could ask Roberta if she could have Emily a bit later than normal."

"I'd like that. Can I come with you when you do your calls? I'd like to see you in action."

He smiled. "Sure." He lifted her hand and kissed her fingers. "Shall we go back to the others? They'll be wondering where we are."

Privately, Fliss thought that everyone would know perfectly well what they'd been up to, but she just nodded. Slowly, holding hands, they walked back through the forest, only releasing hands as they exited the woods and crossed the lawn.

To their credit, the rest of his family didn't comment on the fact that they'd been gone a while. She wasn't sure if he caught the amused smile Elliot gave him, or the way Bianca nudged her twin sister, but if he did, Dominic turned a blind eye and just picked up his guitar and started strumming.

Fliss finished off her wine as the party began to wind down, her emotions entwining throughout her. She couldn't deny a bubbling excitement deep inside at the thought of meeting up with him tomorrow. But she also felt a flutter of nerves. What in hell was she doing, coming on to a Church deacon when she would be going back to LA in a few days? Especially when she was in such a mess? It made no sense at all. The guy had lost his wife, and he was trying to remain true to her—what right did she have to seduce him and break his vows for something that could only ever be a short fling?

And yet, why did it feel so right? She was tired of thinking. Of worrying. Of putting her life into other people's hands. Dominic had kissed her, and it had felt amazing. He was lonely, and although he'd promised his wife that he'd love no other, he was young, and he knew it would be difficult to remain celibate for the rest of his life. She wanted him, and he wanted her. Was there really much more to say about it?

"Ready to go?" Roberta asked her, and she finished off the last mouthful of wine and nodded. They went around saying their goodbyes, and Fliss thanked Noelle for inviting her. When it came to Dominic, she held out her hand, and he chuckled and shook it, his warm skin on hers sending a tingle down her spine.

"See you tomorrow?" she murmured.

He nodded, eyes twinkling. "Until then."

Calling goodbye, Roberta led the way back to the car, and then got in and set off for her house.

It was dark now, especially once they left the town center, the only light coming from oncoming cars or the occasional house.

"Enjoy your little walk tonight?" Roberta asked.

Fliss glanced at her. "Dominic's a nice guy," she said. "I like him a lot."

"He likes you," Roberta said. "I haven't seen him so animated since... well, you know."

Fliss looked out of the window, at the bamboo plants lining the road that towered above them in the darkness. "I said I'd go with him tomorrow when he does his calls. I'd like to find out more about what he does."

"Yeah, why not? I'm sure he'd love the company."

Fliss looked back at her, worry making her stomach churn. "If you rather I didn't see him, I understand. He is your brother, and he's been through a tough time. I'm not trying to make it harder on him."

Roberta smiled, reached out, and took her hand. "I know. I've been telling him for ages that it's time he moved on. I think he's ready, but he's just not met anyone that he'd be willing to move on for, until now. Just... don't break his heart, eh?"

Fliss's eyebrows rose. "Oh my God, of course not. That's the last thing I'd want to do. He knows I'm only here for a few days. Eyes wide open, and all that." She blew out a breath. "Jesus, I'm so sorry, you must think I'm a terrible person. What with everything that's been happening with Jack, and now to come here and flirt with your brother, a deacon, of all people..."

Roberta laughed and returned her hand to the steering wheel. "I perfectly understand you wanting to drown your sorrows, so to speak. And why the hell not? You've obviously made a connection with him that I don't think any of us suspected. What's wrong with a fling? Absolutely nothing, as you say, if everyone's on the same page."

"What's between you and Angus?" Fliss asked, deciding that changing the subject was probably the best option.

Roberta stared at her for a moment. "What do you mean?"

"Aw, come on. I saw the way you looked at him when you thought he wasn't looking."

To her surprise, Roberta's face turned beetroot red. "I didn't."

"Your blush tells me otherwise, Ms. Goldsmith. He seems like a nice guy."

"He also doesn't know I exist."

"What are you talking about? I saw you chatting with him for a good part of the evening."

"Romantically, I mean. I've known him quite a long time, but he's never shown any interest in me."

"So why don't you say something?" Fliss was amused that the forthright Roberta was suddenly shy.

"I'm not going to throw myself at a guy and make an idiot of myself. He's nice enough, but he's nothing special."

Fliss said nothing. She'd seen the way Roberta's eyes had lit up when she'd been talking to Angus, and she'd been fairly certain that she'd caught Angus watching Roberta several times, but the last thing she wanted to do was stick her nose in where it wasn't wanted.

They arrived at the house and went in, poured themselves a glass of wine, and took it out onto the deck, covering their legs with a blanket. Jasmine hopped up onto Roberta's lap, and to Fliss's surprise, Rosie jumped onto hers and curled up. She threaded her fingers through the cat's short silky hair, thinking of how she'd done the same with Dominic when she'd kissed him.

"Do you believe in soul mates?" she asked, stroking the cat's ears.

Roberta rolled her head on the back of the seat to look at her. "Nope."

"Me neither. I think you either get on with someone or you don't. Or, at least, there are degrees of compatibility. What do you want, or expect, from a guy in a relationship?"

Roberta's lips quirked up. "A big cock."

They both burst out laughing. "Fair enough," Fliss replied.

Roberta sighed. "I'm being flippant. Want and expect are two completely different things. I'd like someone who's fun, sexy, thoughtful, caring. Who's good in bed, and willing to find out what I like. Who's intelligent, and who challenges me without steamrolling over me in an argument. Who's loving and kind. But I'm well aware he doesn't exist."

"He might," Fliss said, wondering if she was thinking about Angus.

"I doubt it. When it comes down to it, we're all very selfish creatures, and I can't imagine I'll find someone who's all those things. At the very least, I think faithfulness and honesty are definites, for me.

I couldn't be with someone who didn't think either of those things was important. Everything else is a lottery, you get what you get."

"When did we let the bar sink so low?" Fliss asked sadly.

"It slips an inch every time someone lets us down. It's not to say there aren't good men out there. But nobody's perfect, and it's unrealistic to demand perfection."

"I certainly don't expect it now," Fliss said, "after Jack. Like you said, if someone was faithful, loyal, and honest with me, I think I'd be happy with that. Passion would be lovely, but I'm getting to the stage where contentment would be wonderful. Marriage, a home, kids, a dog… I don't know that I want more than that anymore."

"What about your career? If Whitfield's still interested in having you, what are you going to do?"

"I don't know." Fliss looked out into the darkness. "All I do know is that tonight, out walking with Dominic, I felt more at peace than I've felt in a very long time." She looked across at Roberta then, a little embarrassed. "I'm not saying he's The One or anything—I'm not an idiot."

"I know."

"He's just so easy to be with, and I trust him, which is more than I can say for any other man in my life at the moment."

"I get it," Roberta said. "Being a Church deacon does come with a certain amount of trustability. Is that a word?"

"If it's not, it should be."

"Make the most of him, Fliss. He's had a lot of darkness in his life, what with Jo and then Dad passing. He's had it tough, and I don't see anything wrong with bringing a little light into his day, even if it is only temporary."

Chapter Sixteen

"Don't rush back," Emily said. "You can take as long as you like."

Dominic sent her a wry look as he signaled to turn into Roberta's drive. "I get the message, Em." She'd spent the past twenty minutes trying to wheedle more time at her aunt's. Dominic didn't mind. He knew Roberta loved having her there, maybe seeing herself in her niece at that age. The two of them spent hours cooking, sewing, and making glitter pictures while they watched Disney movies.

He pulled up outside the house, and they both got out. Emily picked up her school bag and they walked up the path together.

"Have a nice time with Fliss," Emily said. "Tell her you like her shoes."

"I don't know anything about women's shoes. Why would I tell her that?"

"Girls like that."

He gave her a suspicious look, but at that moment Roberta opened the door, and Emily ran up and threw her arms around her waist.

"Hello, Monkey!" Roberta kissed the top of her head.

"Hey, Bobcat! We made scones at school today. Kaia burned hers but mine were just right."

"Cool! I thought we'd make fairy cakes this afternoon. We can ice them with all different colors and toppings."

Emily jumped up and down and ran inside, and Roberta smiled. She turned her bright gaze to her brother. "Afternoon."

"Hey." He shoved his hands in his pockets. "Fliss ready?"

"Just about." Her eyes gleamed. "Don't do anything I wouldn't do."

"Wouldn't dream of it."

She grinned. "Got plenty of protection?" He gave her an exasperated look, and she laughed. "Seriously, though," she added, "if you end up wanting me to have Emily overnight, that's fine. I can drop her off to school on the way to work tomorrow."

"I don't know that that's a good idea. She's already trying to match us up."

"What's wrong with that?"

"She's seven, Rob. If she thinks we've... you know, she'll have us married off and roses around the door in no time. I don't want her being disappointed."

Roberta nodded. "Fair enough. Although I don't think it's a bad thing for her to know that there's nothing wrong with her father finding comfort with another woman."

"She's the one trying to convince me."

"Ha! Okay."

Dominic went to reply, but then Fliss appeared behind her, saying goodbye to Emily, and his words melted away on his tongue. She wore jeans and a loose white tunic, she'd caught her hair up in a messy bun, and her face looked fresh and clean of makeup, but she radiated beauty. She was wrong, he thought—she didn't have to turn on a light, it was always there, but it was obviously related to how happy she felt. As she saw him, she lit up, and he felt an answering tug of pleasure inside.

"Hi," she said, coming through the door to stand beside him. Her turquoise eyes glowed brighter than ever.

"Hi." He felt a rush of heat at the thought of her coming back to his place after he'd done his rounds. He couldn't believe he was this lucky.

"See you later," Roberta said. "Have fun."

Fliss sent her a look, but Roberta just laughed and closed the door.

"Sorry," Fliss said as they walked back to the car and got in.

"Don't worry, I've been getting it too. Emily tells me I'm supposed to compliment you on your shoes. I have no idea why."

"Sounds like she's been watching *The American President*," she said with a smile.

"Oh, I knew I'd heard it somewhere." He sighed and started the car. "Little minx." He pulled away and headed into town.

Feeling Fliss's gaze on him, he glanced across at her.

"Just admiring the view," she said.

His lips curved. "Well, thank you."

"You're wearing your collar."

"'Cause I'm working. Is it putting you off?"

"Um... no... but if I think about doing naughty things with you, does that mean I'm going to hell?"

"Probably."

"Fair enough."

They both laughed. Dominic reached out a hand, and Fliss slipped hers into it.

"Any news from back home?" he asked.

Her smile faded. "Not really. No sign of the other photos, so I'm hoping Jack's having second thoughts. My agent's pushing me to go back, of course, but I'm not ready yet."

Dominic felt a rush of relief at that news. "I have you for a few more days?"

She smiled. "I think so."

"Then let's not talk about it."

She nodded, looking relieved. "Where are we off to?"

"The hospice has an open house on Monday afternoons, and I often drop in, in case anyone wants to chat. They're very good at understanding that a dying person's relatives need support as much as the sick person. Are you sure you want to come, though? I can drop you off in town if you'd rather do some shopping."

"Of course I want to come. My grandmother died last year, so I know how important it is to have support for the family. I'd love to watch you at work. As long as they won't mind me being there."

"No, not at all. They might rope you in to make tea or something, though."

"I'm sure I can cope with that."

Dominic hoped he'd done the right thing as he pulled into the long drive leading to the hospice buildings. Fliss appeared kind and understanding, but he had no idea how she would cope with the kind of work he had to do.

Jo had seemed born into it, gifted with a natural urge to please and to serve others. Sometimes, just sometimes, he'd wondered whether it had grown from a desire to feel needed. Which was understandable, and he'd admired her dedication to duty, but occasionally he'd felt that she would rather be visible in the community than at home with him and Emily.

They arrived at the hospice, which consisted of a collection of low wooden buildings incorporating the offices where all the admin staff worked who organized fundraising and the day-to-day running of the place, and behind that a large meeting hall surrounded by smaller counselling rooms. Today the hall was about half full, and he recognized several faces from the Church. Many of them were volunteers, some bringing homemade cakes and biscuits for visitors, others making tea and coffee. There was a little library, and groups of tables and chairs for people to sit and chat or play board games or cards for the afternoon. There was always a nurse or two from the local surgery available for consultation, and two counselors, as well as himself.

Just like the school fair, he thought, it must have looked trivial to a movie star who was used to high society, billionaires, and famous people. But Fliss smiled and shook hands as he introduced her as a friend of his sister who was staying with them for a while. And when one of his parishioners asked if she could talk to him, Fliss went over to the kitchen, and the next thing he knew she was buttering rolls and chatting to the old women there as if they were good friends.

He tore his gaze away from her, and for the next two hours, tried to concentrate on the people who came to him for advice and consolation. He was vaguely aware of Fliss moving around the room, talking to people, and at one point he saw her playing cards with three old guys who were clearly captivated by the gorgeous young woman. He hoped she wasn't too bored, but there wasn't much he could do about it, so he focused on the person sitting opposite him and gave them all his attention until it was time to go.

They waved goodbye and headed back to the car. "Do you need to visit anyone?" Fliss asked as they got in.

He clipped in his seatbelt. "No, I'm done for the day. I'll do my rounds tomorrow." He went to start the engine, then sat back and glanced across at her. "You were great in there."

She tucked a strand of hair behind her ear. "That's a lovely thing to say, especially coming from you."

"What do you mean?"

She gave him an affectionate smile. "You really have no idea, do you?" At his blank stare, she reached up and stroked his cheek. "You are the nicest man alive, Deacon Dom. You gave every person who sat with you in that room one-hundred percent of your attention. You have such a large heart. I feel honored to have met you, and to be friends with you."

Not knowing what to say, he just stared at her, touched beyond words.

After glancing across at the buildings, making sure they weren't being watched, she leaned toward him and pressed her lips to his.

Dominic inhaled, closed his eyes, and focused on the kiss. Her mouth was incredibly soft as it teased his, and when she brushed her tongue across his lip, she tasted of the peppermint slice she'd had that afternoon. He was used to keeping his emotions, his desires, under control, but for the first time in ages he gave into his need for her, cupping her head and plunging his tongue into her mouth. She moaned deep in her throat, a sound so sexy he was hard in seconds, and it was with some difficulty that he eventually pulled away to look down at her helplessly.

She didn't look apologetic or regretful or worried. Instead, she just smiled and whispered, "Take me back to your place."

Wordlessly, he started the car, backed out of the car park, and headed toward the house. His heart raced as he drove, and he was barely aware of the other cars on the road as his mind tortured him with fantasies of what lay ahead.

He felt such a swirl of emotions—excitement, anticipation, and guilt all twisting inside him. He was taking another woman back to the house he'd shared with his wife. He'd walked around that morning while Emily was having her breakfast and had quietly removed the half-a-dozen photos of Jo displayed, feeling huge waves of guilt as he did so. But he'd been unable to take down the large photo of the three of them in the hallway, knowing that Emily would spot it, and feeling too bad at the thought that he was trying to wipe the memory of Jo from the place.

When they'd married, they'd decided to find a home in town, knowing they'd want to get involved in the local community. They'd chosen a house on a quiet road only ten minutes' walk from the high street, and fifteen minutes' walk in the other direction to the church that overlooked the Kerikeri inlet. The house was at the end of the road, surrounded by poplars to give some privacy, and he turned onto the drive and drew up outside, wondering if any of the neighbors had seen them arrive.

He switched off the engine, looking at the house, remembering the first time he'd pulled up here with Jo. They'd been so young—only twenty, convinced they had fifty or sixty years together. They'd fallen in love with the brick-built house, with its large modern kitchen, its light-filled living room, and the south-facing garden that Jo had had such plans for.

He flexed his hand. He'd also removed his wedding ring that morning. His fingers felt bare, light without the weight. He felt guilty about it, but he'd needed to do it, to unchain himself from the past. He couldn't make love to another woman while wearing his wedding ring.

"Dominic," Fliss said, reaching out and startling him out of his reverie. "Are you okay?"

He forced his lips into a smile. "Of course."

"Honey, if you feel too awkward taking me in there, I understand. I don't want you to feel bad."

He focused on her face, on her bright eyes, on her pink lips with the perfect Cupid's bow, and blew out a long, slow breath. "I'm okay. As long as you don't think it's weird."

"You were married, Dom. You shared a house with her. I know she'll have a presence there. And that's okay—she's a big part of your life. I'm not expecting you to discard her as if she's a coat you no longer need. Why don't we go in and you can show me around, and if it feels too odd, we can call it a day?"

Dominic couldn't believe she was being so understanding. He'd thought that if he were ever to bring a woman back to the house, she'd get upset or annoyed at finding photographs or things that his wife had bought. But then Fliss wasn't like any other woman. He was beginning to realize that.

They got out, walked up the path, and he unlocked the door and opened it, stepping aside to let her pass. Fliss went into the cool interior, paused to slip off her shoes, then walked up to the large photograph hanging on the wall.

Dominic closed the door, took off his shoes, and stood beside her.

"She was very beautiful," Fliss said.

Dominic studied the face he knew so well. Jo hadn't been beautiful in the classic way that Fliss was, but she'd had Maori blood going back a few generations, and it had been evident in her light-brown skin, her chocolate-brown eyes, and her thick, dark hair. He'd loved her so much, but she'd been gone for two years now. He'd spent hours gazing at this photo, missing her, longing for her. But today, for the first time since she'd died, he felt nothing but hope that she was somewhere peaceful, and a kind of resignation that that period of his life was done, and it was time to move onto something new.

He looked at Fliss, smiled, took her hand, and led her along the hallway.

Chapter Seventeen

Dominic led Fliss into the living room, and she walked across to the sliding glass doors that overlooked the garden. He'd mentioned that he'd let the garden overrun a little, and she could see that in the untended bushes, the untidy borders, and the longish grass that needed clipping around the edges. She turned and glanced around the living room, seeing the same thing mirrored there. He probably had a cleaner in, she thought, who dusted the tabletops and vacuumed where they walked. The place felt comfortable and cozy, and it was tidy enough, but she could feel the lack of a woman's presence. In spite of the bright colors of the cushions, the pretty paintings on the wall, and the fact that the place was filled with light, it felt... sad.

She turned back to Dominic, who was standing with his hands in the pockets of his trousers, watching her.

"It's a lovely place," she said. "I'm sure you were very happy here."

He didn't say anything, and she walked up to him and cupped his face in her hands. He'd kissed her at the river, and he'd made the mental decision to move on, but he was worried about being here with her, in this house, with the memories of his wife all around them. But they couldn't go to a motel or a B&B, not when he knew everyone in town. And there was no time to drive hundreds of miles to somewhere he wouldn't be recognized.

It was all crazy and it made no sense, but somehow Fliss knew that she was supposed to be with this man, right now, in this house. It was such a strong feeling that she couldn't shake it. Everything that had happened—what Jack had done, hearing from Roberta, coming to New Zealand—had led her to this point. Dominic had been living in the shadows for too long, and he needed bringing back to the light. Her presence here was no more substantial than the shaft of sunlight on the carpet, but instinctively she knew it was going to be enough to banish the darkness.

She looked into his eyes, seeing his need there, his desire, reached up onto her tiptoes, and pressed her lips to his.

Dominic sighed, and then his arms came around her, pulling her against him. She opened her mouth to the brush of his tongue, and heat flowed through her as he deepened the kiss, making her nipples tighten and sending tingles through everywhere else.

"I want you," she whispered against his lips, catching his bottom lip between her teeth and tugging it.

He gave an answering growl, turned her, and backed her up against the wall, which she met with a bump that made her gasp. He didn't apologize, though, just took her hands and pinned them above her head, kissing her again.

Fliss moaned, taken aback by the move, and feeling a wave of desire for this man as he pressed up to her, his body hard against hers. She could feel his erection, proof that he wanted her, that he wanted this, and with a surge of happiness she hooked a leg around his hips and rocked against him.

Lifting his head, he looked down at her, and she flexed her fingers. "Let me go," she whispered. He did so, and she grasped the hem of her top, lifted it over her head, and let it drop to the floor.

Dominic's gaze dropped to drink in the sight of her in her pretty white teddy, the stretchy lace clinging to her curves and the cups outlining her breasts. She laughed at the helpless look on his face, lifting her hands to start unbuttoning his shirt.

"I'm tempted to ask you to keep the collar on," she teased. "But I think for this first time, it's probably better that we take it off."

Lips curving up, he undid the back and removed it, tossing it onto the nearby armchair. She undid the last button and pushed his shirt off his shoulders, letting it fall to the floor. "Mmm," she murmured with approval as she smoothed her hands across his chest, "you have a magnificent body."

"Thank you." He sounded amused, undoing her jeans. They fell to the floor too, and he picked the items up and dropped them onto the chair.

She leaned back against the wall, letting him drink his fill, then accepted his kiss as he pressed against her again. His mouth was harder this time, claiming rather than asking as he let loose his passion, and she sank a hand into his hair, scraping her nails gently against his scalp and enjoying his answering shudder.

His hands fumbled at the waist of his trousers and then they, too, joined the pile of clothes, along with his socks as he flicked them off. Now he was just in his boxer-briefs, black and tight as he'd promised. They were sexy, but she wanted him naked, so she pulled the elastic over his prominent erection and peeled the briefs down his legs, tossing them away when he'd stepped out of them. Keeping her eyes on his, she licked the palm of her hand slowly from the heel to the tip of her fingers. Then, taking his erection in her hand, she began to stroke him.

He leaned his hands on the wall, his lips just brushing hers as he breathed deeply, obviously enjoying the touch.

"Is that nice?" she whispered, squeezing a little before continuing to stroke up and down.

He didn't reply, just looked at her, eyelids at half mast, his hot breath whispering over her lips.

"Want me to stop?" she asked innocently.

His lips curved up, and before she could stop him, he placed both hands beneath her butt and lifted her. Squealing, she wrapped her legs around him, and he laughed as he carried her across to the sofa. Turning, he sat, pulling her astride him, and she slid down his thighs until his erection pressed against her lower stomach.

"You look amazing," he said, moving his hands up from her ribcage to finally cup her breasts. Fliss watched him, enjoying his admiration, murmuring her approval as he brushed his thumbs across her nipples through the lace.

Leaning forward, she kissed his forehead, his temple, his cheekbone, his nose, and then his lips, and he lifted his face, a deep groan sounding in his throat as she slid her tongue against his and kissed him deeply. *Ohhh...* she wanted this man, the hunger growing within her until she felt filled with heat. When he slid the straps of her teddy over her shoulders, exposed a breast, and closed his mouth over a nipple, she clenched her hands in his hair and arched into him, aching with need.

"Dominic..." she whispered, desperate to have him inside her. He slid her other strap down and sucked that nipple too, swapping from one to the other until her breaths came in deep gasps. Moving a hand down to her waist, he caught the elastic edge of her teddy in his fingers, slid his hand expertly over her hip and stomach, and slipped his fingers down into her. She looked into his eyes as he stroked her there, his fingers sliding easily through her folds, and her eyelids fluttered shut when he circled his thumb over her clit, massaging the swollen button.

Without another word, she reached across and picked up the purse she'd left at the end of the sofa, extracted a condom, and tore off the wrapping. Then she held it up for him.

"Are you sure?" she asked.

He took it from her and gave her a wry look. Relieved that he hadn't changed his mind, she moved back enough to let him roll it on, and then she pulled the bottom of the teddy aside and moved so the tip of his erection just entered her. Kissing him, she did her best to relax and sank slowly all the way down until she was impaled on him.

"*Aaahhh.*" His breath mingled with hers, and they sat there like that for a moment, reveling in the feeling of being as one.

She slid her hands into his hair. "You feel good."

"You feel amazing."

"No regrets?" she whispered.

He shook his head, held her hips, and pushed up, swelling inside her. She moaned and rocked her hips, forcing him to slide in and out.

Dominic's breath hissed between his teeth. Fliss continued to move, keeping her gaze on his, occasionally kissing him. It was slow and sensual and sexy, a gradual exploration of one another, as he stroked his hands down her back and up over her breasts, and she brushed her fingers over his biceps, his shoulders, and the defined muscles of his chest.

"Mmm… I could do this forever," she said with a sigh, skating her lips over his and shuddering as sexy shivers rippled through her.

"You like it slow?" he asked, his voice husky.

She touched her nose to his and ran her tongue along his bottom lip. "Slow and sexy… hot and hard… Either's fine by me."

In answer, he slung an arm around her waist, heaved up, and tipped her onto her back on the floor, still inside her.

"Ooh!" she said with a gasp. "Wow, that was impressive."

"Needed a bit more room." He shifted to make himself comfortable, then bent and kissed her.

"Mmm." She looked up into his bright green eyes, her heart thumping as he began to move properly, thrusting hard inside her.

"Holy shit." Fliss felt a rush of excitement and wrapped her legs around his hips. He'd been so hesitant that she'd been convinced she'd have to guide him all the way, and she was thrilled that he'd taken charge. He certainly seemed to have overthrown his worries, screwing her on her back on his carpet. "Are you sure this is allowed in your line of work?" she asked, panting.

He chuckled and kissed up her jaw to her ear. "If it's not, I'm happy to quit."

She groaned as he nipped her earlobe. "Now I know you're teasing me."

"Right at this moment, I couldn't give a shit about the day job." He pushed her knee higher and gave an ecstatic sigh as he sank into her.

"Oh... Dominic..."

"I'm crazy about you, you know that?" He said the words as he looked into her eyes, and she melted inside.

"I'm nothing special," she said, her voice catching with her emotion.

He slowed for a moment, a frown flickering on his brow, and kissed her again. "That couldn't be further from the truth."

"Are you trying to make me cry?"

He kissed her eyelids, her nose, and her mouth again. "Absolutely not. Now, I'm going to make you come. If that's okay with you?" His mouth quirked up.

She swallowed down her emotion, looking into his eyes as he began to thrust properly again, pushing down with each movement of his hips so that he ground against her clit. *Ohhh...* he was good at this; she wasn't going to have to help him along at all. Lifting her arms above her head, she stretched out beneath him and let her thighs fall open, abandoning herself completely as the first tingles of an orgasm began to thread through her.

Dominic lifted up onto his hands and thrust harder, and she shuddered as everything clenched deep inside and came hard—strong, powerful pulses that had her crying out loud. He paused, waiting for her to finish, and she knew he must be watching her, because he'd be the sort of guy who would enjoy giving pleasure as much as taking it.

Not that he wasn't prepared to take it either... As she flopped back with a groan, he began to move again, short, quick thrusts that told her he wasn't far from coming. She opened her mouth to his kiss, sliding her arms around his back so she could feel his muscles moving beneath her fingers, and dug her nails in, causing him to exclaim.

"Come on," she said, "fuck me harder, I know you want to."

He groaned and did so, his hips meeting her thighs with a sharp smack, and she sank her fingers into his hair and pulled his head down to kiss him, delving her tongue into his mouth. He was close, so close, and she let him lift up so she could watch him, and saw the moment his climax took him—the way his brow creased, his muscles turned rigid, and his body shuddered as he spilled inside her.

"Fuck," he said, "*aaahhh* fuck."

She stroked his face, his back, murmuring her approval, enjoying every millisecond of his pleasure. And when he'd finally done, she gave a wistful sigh, half wishing it could have gone on forever.

He withdrew, lowered onto the carpet, and gathered her up in his arms. "Ah, Fliss. That was amazing."

"Mmm." She snuggled up beside him. Luckily, the carpet had thick pile and it wasn't too uncomfortable. "It was. For a churchman, you're pretty good in the sack."

He snorted. "The kind of things I was thinking, I'm definitely going to hell."

"Aw. Well, if there's no pleasure in heaven, I don't want to go anyway."

He gave a short laugh and kissed her forehead. "Me neither. I don't believe that sex and pleasure is evil. I think the person who suggested that wasn't getting any."

She giggled, and he grinned at her. "You're very irreverent at times," she said.

"The Irreverent Reverend is going to be my new title."

They both started laughing, the warm sun streaming over them, turning them to gold.

Chapter Eighteen

Dominic could have lain on the carpet all night with her, but after a while he worried that she was going to get cold or sore, so he rose and lifted her up, and pulled on his boxers and trousers. When he turned, to his surprise she'd taken off her teddy and she was wearing his shirt. He'd seen women do that in the movies, but Jo had never done it.

"Am I supposed to wear your top?" he asked, picking up the flimsy piece of material. "I don't think it'll fit. I'll end up doing a Hulk impersonation."

"You're fine topless," she said, coming up and resting her hands on his chest. Her fingers splayed, stroking across his skin, her thumbs brushing his flat nipples.

He caught her hands, held them in his own, then moved them slowly behind her back and held them there. She tugged, realized he wasn't going to let her go, and lifted her amused gaze to his. "Don't tell me the naughty preacher likes to play tie-me-up."

"I can think of a thousand-and-one things I'd like to do with you." He kissed her cheekbone, her jaw, and around to her ear, enjoying the way she shivered, her nipples peaking through his cotton shirt. "You've brought me back to life," he murmured, holding both her wrists with one hand. He brought the other around to unpop a button of the shirt and slipped his hand beneath to cup her breast. They exchanged a long, sensual kiss, which was interrupted only when her stomach gave a loud rumble.

Laughing, he lifted his head.

"I'm so sorry," she said, blushing. "How embarrassing. I skipped lunch."

"Well, that won't do." He released her hands and kissed her forehead. "We should get something to eat. I'm sure Emily's told you I'm a terrible cook. Would you like to go out to dinner?" He turned to pick up an empty cup that he'd left on the table that morning, squashing the flicker of worry at the thought of anyone seeing him in a restaurant with a woman.

"It's up to you," she said. "If you'd rather take me back to Roberta's now, I don't mind. I've had a lovely time, and I'm not expecting to be wined and dined."

He turned back to her then. "You deserve to be," he said, somewhat fiercely, cupping her face with a hand. "I didn't just bring you here to have sex with you and then send you home."

"It's okay." She looked amused. "I didn't expect more than that."

No, why would she? She was going back to the US in a few days. There wasn't time for a relationship to develop. She recognized this for what it was—a coming together—literally—in an hour of need, and she saw nothing wrong with that. How wonderful to be so free.

Tipping her head to the side, she studied his face, her turquoise eyes kind. "Poor Dominic," she murmured, "so caught up in guilt and shame and worry. You said you didn't think there was anything wrong with pleasure."

"I don't, as such, but I've never done anything like this before. I'd hate you to feel as if I've used you."

"If that's the case, I've used you too."

"Hmm. I suppose."

"But I don't think the word used comes into it at all. We shared a moment, and it was wonderful. I don't want you to think I do this all the time—I've had a few relationships, but I don't sleep around, and I certainly didn't plan for this to happen while I was away. But I think we saw a need in each other, and we were able to fulfil that need. What's so terrible about that?"

"Nothing." He stroked her cheek.

"You're bound to feel differently about things, because of Jo, and because of your faith. And that's okay. Just… try not to regret it. That will make me sad."

He kissed her, a gentle press of his lips to hers. "Never." She opened her mouth to him, and he dipped his tongue inside, sighing at the slick, sweet taste of her. He wanted to tell her that it wasn't about regretting what he'd done. It was about wanting more.

But it was dumb to go down that road. This was just a fling, and it would be pointless to talk or even think about anything more.

That didn't mean she had to go right away, though.

"Roberta said she's happy for Emily to stay the night," he said. He took her bottom lip between his teeth and tugged it gently. "So you can stay, if you like. If we only have the one night, we might as well make the most of it."

She slid her arms around him, her lips curving up. "You mean I haven't worn you out?"

"There's life in the old dog yet."

"In that case, I'm definitely staying."

He laughed and kissed her nose. "But first, food!"

"Why don't I cook us something?" she asked. "It seems a shame to go out when we're all nice and comfortable."

"You can't stay at my house and then have to do the cooking."

"Why not?"

He frowned.

"We all have different strengths," she said, walking toward the kitchen. "Yours might not be cooking, but you have definite advantages in other areas." She winked at him over her shoulder.

He grinned. "I'm glad you think so."

"Oh, most definitely. Now, you sit there, and I'll put something together." She directed him to a stool in front of the breakfast bar and started looking in the cupboards. "You obviously like pasta." She ran her fingers over the packets of penne, shells, macaroni, and spaghetti. "What do you normally have with it?"

"Tomato sauce out of a jar."

"All right. Let's do something different." She opened the fridge, surveyed the contents, and took out some cheese, a pack of ham, and some eggs. "I'll make a carbonara."

Dominic rang Roberta to ask her to have Emily for the night, then watched Fliss as she chopped and cooked, listening to her sing while she worked. She brought color and light into a house that he hadn't realized until that moment had become dull and gray, like finding a scarlet flower growing in the middle of a wintry city.

How strange that only days ago he hadn't even known she was coming to Kerikeri. Roberta had mumbled something about it, but he'd been busy and hadn't connected her visitor with the girl from his childhood.

When the dish was ready, he poured them both a glass of Pinot Gris, and they ate up at the breakfast bar.

"What made you decide to become a counselor?" Fliss asked, twirling a strand of tagliatelle into a ball with her fork. "Were you inspired by a therapist you had when you were young?"

"No, nothing like that. I never had the need for therapy growing up. But I was always involved with the community. I was a prefect at the high school, and I helped out a lot with the younger kids. I started to realize how the ones who misbehaved were generally those who came from the more difficult backgrounds. They often talked to me— it just sort of happened naturally. It was one of the sports teachers who asked if I'd thought about going on to take a counseling course at university. I hadn't, but after he'd mentioned it I couldn't get it out of my head."

"You do seem to have a knack with people. You have a very calming influence."

"I've been told that a lot."

"It's a rare gift," she said, "to make someone feel as if they're the only person in the world when you're talking to them. As if they're special."

"I believe they are. That probably helps." He took another mouthful of the creamy pasta. "This is very good."

"Thank you. Do you ever feel as if it's all pointless? That no matter how many people you help, there are always thousands, millions, more?"

He sipped some wine. "No, you can't think like that. Even those people who travel to Africa to build schools or feed the hungry can't save everyone. All we can do is help one person at a time, the best way we can."

She poked at a piece of ham with her fork. "With Elliot being a cop, and Angus a doctor, and Rafe a firefighter… does it seem odd to you that other people do ordinary jobs that don't involve helping people all the time?"

"No, of course not. I wouldn't presume to judge someone else's path. My sisters run a bridal shop and café, so they're not exactly saving the world. But they bring a huge amount of pleasure to people, and that's no small feat. You're the same. Movies help people escape their troubles, and everyone has to earn a living."

She swirled her wine in her glass, studying him with a small smile. "You're very kind."

"Life's hard enough without having other people judge you all the time. All each of us can do is try to live our lives the best we can and be honest with ourselves."

She sucked her bottom lip, her gaze dropping to her plate, and she pushed the pasta around for a while.

"What?" he asked softly. "What did I say?"

She gave him a bright smile. "Nothing. It's not you. For some time now, I haven't felt as if my life has held any… value, I suppose. By most people's standards, I'm successful. I make good money, I get to go to parties, and I meet famous people. I know I'm lucky compared to so many people in this world, who aren't loved, and who don't have enough to eat."

"But you're not happy."

She didn't say anything.

"You can talk to me," he said. "I'm not going to tell anyone."

"It's not that. I feel ashamed."

"Why?"

"Because you're a good man doing great things, and I feel about an inch high sitting here complaining because my life's not going exactly the way I want."

He reached out and took her hand. "It doesn't work like that. You have your own path, and you have decisions to make. Forks in the road. You're being challenged at the moment, forced to reassess where you are and what you want in the future. That's a good thing. Life's waking you up, giving you a slap around the face. You might come out of it thinking how lucky you are and deciding to make the most of the opportunities you have. Or you might decide to put it all behind you and move on to something new. It's exciting, don't you think? All those choices."

She gave a little laugh, her eyes shining. "Do you see good in everyone and everything?"

"Maybe I do. There's always hope."

"Faith, hope, and love?"

"And the greatest of these…" He pulled her toward him, off the stool, and she rose and moved into his embrace. She wrapped her arms around his neck and buried her face there.

"I love the way you make me feel," she whispered. "Like a diamond."

"I was thinking you're more like a flower in a city," he said. "A touch of beauty amongst all the concrete and steel."

"I'm so glad I met you." She moved back a little and looked up at him.

Man, she was beautiful. He moved his hands to the few buttons on the shirt that were done up, undid them, and slid his hands onto her warm skin.

"Mmm," she murmured, lifting her face to his kiss. He delved his tongue into her mouth, skating his hands up over her ribs to cup her breasts, and she sighed against his mouth when he brushed his thumbs over her nipples. They were swollen and soft, but tightened under his touch, making him hard as a rock in seconds.

At that moment, his phone rang.

They stopped, and Fliss lifted her head with a sigh.

"Sorry," he said, cursing the caller in his head. "I should get that."

"Of course."

Reluctantly, he picked up the phone and answered it. "Hello?"

"It's me," Elliot said. "Is Fliss with you?"

He glanced at her. "Yeah. And it's not a great time for a chat…"

"You can put a sock on the door later. Something's happened."

Dominic frowned. "What?"

"The photos are out."

"What photos?"

"The photos of Fliss," Elliot said impatiently. "Her ex has released them, and the video. It's just breaking now on Celebrity Scene—Karen spotted it. I thought you ought to know."

Dominic looked at Fliss, who had paled at the mention of the word photos. "What?" she whispered. "What's happened?"

"Okay," he said to Elliot. "Thanks."

"No worries. Let me know if you need me."

"Will do." Dominic hung up, then took her hands. "That was Elliot," he said slowly.

She bit her lip hard, trembling. "He's done it, hasn't he," she said. "Jack. He's released the photos."

He nodded, wishing he could save her from this. "I'm so sorry."

"Oh my God." She covered her face with her hands. "What am I going to do?"

Chapter Nineteen

Fliss pushed away from Dominic and walked over to her purse to grab her phone.

"Don't," he said, following her, but she backed away from him, turning the phone on.

"I have to look. I want to know what he said." Her heart pounding, she went over to the sliding doors to the garden and waited for the phone to power up. Immediately, it started pinging with notifications, messages, and texts from her agent, her mother, and acquaintances—she couldn't really call them friends, as she knew they were only phoning to rubberneck and see how she was reacting to the news of the photos being out there.

She checked her emails, pulled up the first one from her agent, which had the link to the Celebrity Scene website, and clicked on it.

Dominic had joined her at the window, his hands in the pockets of his trousers, not trying to stop her again. She glanced up at him, then down at the screen as the site loaded.

Yes, there they were, on the home page, under a huge headline, Rivers Runs Deep. She scrolled down, turning so Dominic could see the screen.

"You don't have to show me," he said.

"I want you to see." Her eyes felt hot and scratchy, and her stomach churned. How come only a few minutes ago she'd felt happier than she'd ever felt before in her life?

The photos popped up. There were seven in all, various shots of her in the bedroom and bathroom. In six of them she was wearing a thin dressing gown tied loosely in the middle. She'd been getting ready to go to a party that evening, and Jack had snapped her as she'd walked around and brushed her hair, catching her unguarded, laughing, giving him a scolding look. In the last photo, the gown was open, exposing her from breast to thigh, revealing a pair of tiny black panties.

Dominic said nothing as she scrolled down, revealing the photos.

She got to the bottom, and there was the promised video. She pressed play, her heart in her mouth. Jack had obviously taken it a few moments after the last photo, and it was a ten-second video of her dancing for him, twirling in a circle, her arms above her head as she walked toward him in a sultry fashion, her breasts swaying.

She blew out a shaky breath. It wasn't a sex tape as she'd feared. But it was bad enough. The end of the article talked about how she'd gone into hiding, with lots of speculation as to where she might be. Wellington was mentioned, but although the press appeared to be watching her mother's house, there had obviously been no sight of her.

She looked up at Dominic. He was leaning against the glass, his expression carefully blank.

"I suppose you're wondering what all the fuss is about," she whispered. "I've had near-naked scenes in some of my movies, and this isn't really any worse than that."

"Of course it is," he said. "Because you let him take these thinking they would be for his eyes only. You didn't give him permission for them to be splashed all over the internet."

Her eyes filled with tears. "I thought he loved me."

Dominic sighed and pulled her into his arms. "Come here." He folded his big strong arms around her, and she put her face in her hands and cried.

After a few moments, he bent and slid an arm beneath her knees and lifted her easily into his arms. He carried her through to the other side of the house and into the main bedroom, and climbed onto the bed with her, leaning back on the pillows with her curled on his lap.

They sat like that for a long time, her tears gradually subsiding, to be replaced by a dull tiredness. Outside, the sun had set, and the garden was sinking gradually into darkness. Stars began popping out on the sky as it turned from blue to purple to black, Sirius twinkling brightly above them. The moon was nearly full, and with some surprise she realized it was upside down compared to the northern hemisphere. Of course it would be. Why had she not noticed it before?

Dominic held her quietly, stroking her back with a hand. "There's something so calming about you," she said quietly, conscious of the rhythmic thud of his heart beneath her hand. "You make me feel as if nothing outside this room should matter." She frowned. "No, that's not right, not that it shouldn't matter, but that it's pointless to expend energy worrying about things over which you have no control."

"I guess I do feel like that. There are many things I could get angry at, if I chose. But I don't want to spend the rest of my life angry at the world."

"I admire that. I wish I could be the same, but it's hard to put into practice. I feel so many emotions at the moment and I can't control them."

"What do you feel?" he wanted to know.

"Furious. Ashamed. Disappointed. Hurt."

"All right, let's go through them. Furious at Jack?"

"Yes. And at myself for getting in this position. Kurt—my agent—warned me not to let men take photos of me. It's true that Jack took me by surprise, you can see that in the photos, but even so, I should have told him to delete them."

"All right. Why ashamed? As you said, you've done near-naked shots in movies. It was clear that he caught you unawares. And a human body is nothing to be ashamed about."

His hand stroked her back, and she let the words settle in, like a stone sinking into a vat of treacle. "You're right. And I'm conscious that it's a first world problem. In the big scheme of things, flashing a boob on the Internet isn't the end of the world. Nobody's died or been physically hurt. And it could also have been a lot worse—I was worried that it was a sex tape. But it's the... scandal, I suppose. My dad died when I was ten, but I'm sure he would've been horrified at what's happened. So will my grandparents. Baring a bit of skin on camera in a controlled environment is one thing, being betrayed like this is another. I feel... violated. Is that ridiculous?"

"Of course not. Any time you put your trust in someone and they betray that trust it's going to do damage. It's no surprise that you feel hurt. Especially if you loved him."

"I did," she said. "Or I thought I did, anyway. We only dated for five months, but I thought it was serious. I trusted him. I can't believe he would do this to me. But then I never thought he'd kiss another woman, either. They say love is blind, don't they? I suppose much of it is fabrication in our heads. I made up this big fantasy of how perfect we were for one another and conjured up a persona for him that he was never going to live up to."

"I don't think you should put yourself down because you hoped he wouldn't cheat on you. It's not too much to ask, Fliss."

She wiped her face, cross with herself for crying, and leaned her head tiredly on his shoulder. "I wish I'd never moved to Wellington and become an actress. Do you think we'd have dated if I'd stayed?"

"Who knows? Maybe."

"But then you wouldn't have met Jo or had Emily, so that wouldn't be right. I suppose things are meant to happen the way they are." He didn't say anything. "I'm sorry, I didn't mean to upset you," she added.

"You haven't." He lifted her hand and kissed her fingers. "I was thinking about what you said. Whether things are meant to happen the way they do."

"Does the Church believe in Fate?"

"It's not a biblical concept. The Bible teaches us that Man—and Woman—were created with the ability to make moral choices. And that we're responsible for those choices. Whether you believe the story of Adam and Eve is real or just a parable, the point is that they weren't puppets—they had the ability to choose obedience or disobedience with all its consequences. And we're taught that we sin because we choose to. But the Bible also makes it clear in several places that both God and Jesus have pre-arranged plans, so maybe there is a pattern."

"You like theology, don't you?" she asked. "Analyzing religion."

"I do. I took a theology degree and loved every minute of it, because it burrowed right to the roots of everything. I do have faith, but the fascination for me is understanding why people choose to make the decisions they do, and how they deal with the consequences of their actions."

She straightened a little, so she could see his face, just visible in the semi-darkness. "I like that about you," she said softly. "I like that you think deeply about things and weigh up the moral implications of your actions."

"I can see why that would appeal to you at the moment."

"Jo must have worshipped the ground you walked on."

A frown flickered on his brow. "I wouldn't put it like that."

"Why not?" If she were married to a man like this, Fliss knew she would give thanks every day.

"I'm not sure that I lived up to her high standards," he said. "I tried, but I failed frequently."

"I have trouble believing that."

"I'm far from perfect."

"I have trouble believing that, too."

He gave her a wry smile. "Jo had an endless capacity for compassion. If someone was in need, she would put them first, before herself, before her family, sometimes. I've never been like that. If someone's in need, of course I'll do my best to help. But I can be selfish."

"I don't think you have an ounce of selfishness in you," she said.

"I do. I may look like a saint, but you have no idea what I'm saying in my head."

She smiled. "I guess not."

He sighed. "I suppose I'm not that bad. But however hard I tried, I always felt that Jo was... disappointed in me." He stopped and swallowed, looking out at the garden. It had obviously taken a lot for him to admit that, to speak up against his wife.

They were in his marital bed, with memories of Jo all around him like thick mud sucking at his boots, holding him back. And yet he'd brought Fliss home and had made love to her, which she knew was a huge step for him. He was ready to move on. He just needed a bit of help doing so.

He looked back at her and kissed her forehead. "What are you going to do?"

"I don't know." Her heart sank again as she remembered the photos and how Hollywood would be filled with glee at the thought of her in trouble. "I guess Whitfield won't want me now."

"Really? You're going to be frontline news for a while. I would have thought that would only increase your appeal."

"Maybe." She hesitated and bit her lip.

"Go on," he said.

"I know I sound spoilt and precious at the moment."

"But..."

"But I hate it. All the attention. I thought it was what I wanted—fame and stardom, and maybe I did, but not like this. I wanted... admiration, I suppose. To win awards for my movies. To be... loved. Not mocked. I know other people in the business are going to be full of joy when they see what's happening because I've seen them be like it when it's happened to other people. I hate it. All the hypocrisy, the glee, the smugness because it's not happening to them. It's all so... shallow and meaningless. And I hate that it's affecting me like this. I want to rise above it all, but I can't. I feel as if there are invisible hands pulling me down all the time. I don't want to live like this."

Dominic didn't say anything, and they sat there in the darkness while her mind whirred and clicked, going around and around in circles.

"What would you like to do?" he asked eventually. "I've only had one glass of wine. I could take you back to Roberta's, if you want. Would you like to go to Wellington to talk to your mother about it? Or return to LA and confront it all? What do you want, Fliss?"

She looked up at him, at his handsome face lit by the glow of the moon. At his muscular arms and strong shoulders. His green eyes had turned silver in the moonlight, and as she lifted a hand to cup his face, they glinted, sending a little shiver down her back.

"I want you inside me," she whispered, and lifted up to kiss him.

He groaned and kissed her back, delving his tongue into her mouth, and she pushed all thoughts of the photos out of her mind, turning her attention to the man in her arms, his hot mouth, and his young, strong body. It wasn't that long ago they'd had sex, but she was burning for him again, desire rippling through her as he slid his hands under her shirt, skating them over her skin.

"Take me away," she said as he kissed down her neck, her nipples peaking in his searching fingers. "Make me forget."

"Yes ma'am," he said, and then he tipped back onto the bed, pulling her with him, and enfolding her in his arms.

Chapter Twenty

At that moment, Dominic felt like the weakest man on earth. Neither of their motives for sleeping together were pure. He should have insisted that Fliss return to Roberta's, because he knew she was only using him to try to forget the disaster her life had turned into. And he had a heavy feeling in his gut at the thought that his marriage had obviously meant so little, because he'd thrown away all his principles for the opportunity to have sex with a pretty woman. How fucking shallow was that? No amount of talk about finding comfort and sharing and all that crap was enough to take away the truth—that he'd felt the need for sexual release, and Fliss had been convenient.

But as she kissed him, and he stroked his hands over her warm body, he felt the first twinges of indignation. It wasn't all about that. He liked her. He liked the fact that she was angry at her ex, and that she was feeling dissatisfied with her Hollywood life. And he liked the way she looked at him, and how she made him feel. No man was an island entire of itself, he thought, according to Donne, and Dominic had isolated himself for too long. He spent his life in the community, being with people every day, and the deacon was happy with that, but the man had been slowly dying, and Fliss had given him the kiss of life.

He loved the way she kissed him, hungrily, as if she couldn't get enough of him, as if moving her lips away would mean she'd die. Jo had enjoyed lovemaking, but he'd always gotten the feeling that her mind had been elsewhere. After Emily had been born, they'd settled for having sex on a Sunday morning, when he'd dragged her back to bed while Emily was still asleep. It had rarely been more than once a week, and it had turned a bit predictable, in spite of his attempts to make it otherwise.

Presumably, the passion in every relationship faded after a while. He didn't have enough experience to know, having only slept with one woman his whole life. But he'd missed this. The frenzied, urgent desire, the hunger, the being wanted.

Beneath the shirt she wore, he moved his hands over her back and ribs, and up, filling his palms with her breasts. She sighed, and when he tugged her nipples and turned them from soft peaks to tight buttons, she ground against him and moaned.

"I want you," she said fiercely, sliding her hand into his hair, and clenching her fingers. "I want you inside me."

"Patience," he said, pushing her up astride him so he could capture a nipple in his mouth. Man, he'd missed this too, the feel of a woman's nipple against his tongue, the amazing way they reacted to his touch. He teased and sucked and nibbled, moving from one to the other, and Fliss gasped and arched her back, pushing her breasts into his hands.

When neither of them could bear it any longer, she lifted off him so he could remove his clothing, retrieved a condom from her purse, and then returned to sit astride him, still wearing his shirt. He waited for her to pass him the condom, but she bent and kissed him, then pressed her lips to his neck and down his chest, brushing against his hair and flat nipples, then over his stomach, and even lower. He held his breath as she took his erection in her hand, and then he covered his face with his hands as she closed her mouth over the tip.

"Fuck…" he said, the word muffled through his fingers, as white-hot heat spread through him. Returning his hands to the duvet, he looked down at her, turned on by the sight of himself disappearing between her pink lips.

"Mmm…" Fliss lifted her head and licked her lips. "You taste amazing." She dipped her head, sliding her tongue down the shaft, and then took him in her mouth again, sucking hard as she massaged the rest of his erection with her hand.

He bore it as long as he could, tempted to come in her mouth, but a greater part of him wanted to bury himself inside her. So, eventually, he took her arms and pulled her up toward him.

"Aw," she said, rolling the condom down his glistening length. "I was enjoying that."

"I want to fuck you," he said, and she laughed and bent to kiss him.

"For a preacher, you have a dirty mouth." She touched her lips to his. "I love it." Moving her hips, she directed his erection until the tip parted her folds. Then, very slowly, she sank down onto him.

Dominic slid his hands up her thighs, enjoying every second. She was hot and wet, clamped around him, and she looked amazing in his shirt, the front parted to reveal her breasts, the nipples hard in the silvery light. At some point, she'd released the clip in her hair and it hung loose around her shoulders, and her half-lidded eyes gave her a sultry look. She was made for sex, this woman. He'd already taken the step and given into temptation. Why feel guilty now? He might as well make the most of it.

Ignoring what the deacon half of him would say to that comment, he focused on how it felt to slide in and out of her as she rocked her hips. *Aaahhh...* that felt so good... He brushed a hand down her body to between her legs and slid his thumb down to press against her clit. She moaned and tipped her head back, lifting her hands to her breasts to touch her own nipples. He gave a helpless sigh of lust, circling slowly over the soft button with his thumb, enjoying watching himself slipping in and out of her body.

She dropped her head to look at him, her eyes hot with passion. "Oh God, I'm so close..."

"Slow down," he scolded, taking her hands by her wrists, and moving them away from her breasts. "We've only just started."

She tried to pull her hands away, but he held on tight, and she moaned, trying to grind against him. "Please," she whispered.

He let go of her hands and returned his thumb to between her legs. "All right. But that means you're going to come again when I'm ready."

Nibbling her bottom lip with her teeth while he aroused her, she gave him an amused look. "I think the real Dominic's starting to come out to play."

"He's been asleep for far too long," he said, wondering whether he'd ever fully let go with Jo. Lifting up, he pulled Fliss tightly to him and kissed her hard, and she rocked a few times, then came, clenching around him with beautiful deep gasps.

When she'd done, he took the collar of the shirt she was wearing and tugged it halfway down her back. Then, holding her tightly, he twisted on the bed so she was under him. The shirt, caught beneath her, pinned her arms to her sides, and when he lowered down on top of her, she discovered that she was completely immobile.

"Ah," she said as he pushed up her thighs and buried himself deeply inside her. "I didn't expect that."

"Check mate," he said, and kissed down her neck to her breasts.

He spent a long while kissing her nipples, arousing her again, all the while moving slowly, grinding against her clit with every thrust. Fliss moaned, unable to do anything except lie there and accept his kisses, and fuck, if that wasn't more of a turn on than anything else he'd ever done in the bedroom.

"Oh jeez," she said, locking her ankles behind his back as his body started to take over, plunging down into her soft flesh.

"You're going to come again," he said fiercely, so hot for her now that he thought he might self-combust.

"Dominic…" she whispered, but he crushed his lips to hers, and her words turned into a moan. His tongue mimicked the thrust of his hips, and she squirmed beneath him, arching her back. Taking the hint, he kissed her nipples again, and she cried out. "Harder," she whispered. "Fuck me harder. I'm going to come."

He lifted up, adoring this woman, wishing he could do this all day, every day, because she seemed to understand what he needed. He'd not done this for so long, and he couldn't understand why he'd waited, because it was fucking amazing, and she was so hot, so wet, so helpless beneath him. He pounded into her, pushing her up the bed with every thrust, until her head met the headboard and he was holding onto it, losing himself entirely. He was vaguely aware of her crying out and squeezing around him, but all it did was fire him up more. He thrust and he thrust and he thrust, closing his eyes as the pressure built inside him, and then his climax hit him like a truck. He gasped out loud, pushing as deep as he could inside her, feeling a fierce surge of possessiveness as he spilled. She was his completely, his body claiming her in the most basic, animal way possible, and he knew at that moment that he was never going to let anyone hurt her again.

Then the paroxysm passed, leaving him gasping, his chest heaving. He blinked and focused on her, finding her looking up at him, her eyes shining silver in the moonlight, her lips open with wonder.

"Wow," she said. "Holy fuck."

"Yeah." He blew out a breath and rested his forehead on her shoulder. "Please tell me that was as good for you as it was for me."

"I've lost the feeling in both my arms, and my head probably has a lump the size of a walnut, but yeah, that was pretty amazing."

"Jesus." He lifted up hurriedly, but she was already laughing as he withdrew and helped her out of the shirt.

"I'm joking," she scolded, sighing as he tossed the shirt onto the floor. "Oh God." She flopped back onto the bed, her arms above her head. "I'm not kidding, Dominic. That was the best fuck I've ever had."

He laughed and collapsed beside her. "Thank you. I think."

She rolled onto her side and propped her head on a hand, studying his face. "Who'd have thought it? The nice, innocent deacon, turning into an absolute firework in the bedroom."

"Are you trying to make me blush?"

"I'm not mocking you, Dominic. You were amazing. Oh my God. I'm not going to be able to walk for a fortnight."

He looked at her in concern. "I didn't hurt you?"

"God, no. Good sex should always take away your ability to walk. And that was very good sex."

"Will you stop?" he scolded, embarrassed.

"I can't. You were *magnifique*."

"Jesus."

"And now the prim preacher's cursing. I'm really corrupting you."

He covered his face with his hands and groaned.

"Aw." She snuggled closer to him and nibbled his earlobe. "You love it really."

"I do. God help me."

"I really don't understand why you said that Jo didn't worship you. I want to worship the ground you walk on. I'm going to walk a few feet in front of you everywhere now, throwing rose petals."

He lowered his hands, looking up at the ceiling.

"Shit," Fliss said hurriedly, "I'm sorry. That was a terrible thing to say. I didn't mean to mock her."

"You weren't. It's okay." He ran a hand through his hair. "It was never like that with her, that's all."

Her silvery eyes scanned his face, guilty and curious at the same time. "What do you mean?"

"I don't know. Our sex life was good enough. But what I just did would have been... inappropriate, I suppose. She was very self-contained. She didn't like letting go or losing control. Pleasure was one thing, but she would have thought of this as... indulgent."

He stopped, biting his lip. He shouldn't talk about her like that. He was lying in their bed, for Christ's sake. How fucking disloyal could he be in one night?

But Fliss kissed his shoulder, stroked his face, then turned his head toward her. "She was your wife, the mother of your child, and your first love," she said softly. "And you've been nothing but loyal your whole life. There's only me here, honey. It's okay. I understand."

He swallowed hard, closing his eyes as she kissed him, then lifting a hand to hold her head to keep her there.

This was about comfort and desire, an opportune meeting when both of them were adrift and in need, like seeing a lighthouse in the dark.

But it was more than that, too. It wasn't just about sex. Something in this woman spoke to him, right to his heart. She'd crept beneath all the barriers he'd erected around himself and had openly and willingly offered herself to him in a way that had just exploded his world. He was going to remember this moment forever, lying hot and sticky in the dark, her body molded to his, her mouth soft as her tongue teased his lips.

Oh Jesus. How was he ever going to let her go?

Chapter Twenty-One

"Would you like to come and give me a hand with some of the gowns?" Noelle asked. "Phoebe and Bianca are busy, and I'd like to change the displays."

It was early afternoon the following day, and the lunchtime rush was over in the café. Angie was off sick, and Fliss had been serving while Roberta made coffees and Libby did the baking. Fliss had done a fair bit of waitressing when she was younger, so she knew the ropes, and besides, busy in a Kerikeri café was nothing like busy in LA.

Still, she was ready for a break, and after a glance at Roberta, who nodded, she smiled and said, "I'd love to."

Removing her apron, she followed Noelle across the café, through the archway, and into the bridal shop. Even though the connecting doors were open, the shop was cooler and quieter. It was raining outside, but the crystal chandelier in the middle of the shop lit up the interior and made the gowns sparkle.

"I feel as if I've entered a princess's castle in Disneyland." Fliss walked along the line of dresses, brushing the plastic covers with her fingers. "This must be the best job in the world."

"I do love it." Noelle was holding up several gowns by the hangers, apparently debating which ones should be displayed on the mannequins. "I feel like a fairy godmother, granting wishes." She glanced at Fliss and smiled. "Want me to wave my wand for you?"

"That would be wonderful."

"What would you wish for?"

Fliss's eyebrows rose. "Honestly? I'm not sure. Maybe to have made the past week not happen. Not to have met Jack. Although after speaking to Dominic, I've been thinking that even if things happen that aren't pleasant, it's wrong to wish they hadn't happened. It's all part of life, isn't it?"

"It is," Noelle said, and Fliss remembered that she'd lost her husband just over a year ago. She hooked the gowns she was holding onto a peg on the wall and turned the mannequin around. "Can you help me get this dress off?"

"Sure." Fliss began to undo the tiny pearl buttons that ran down the back of the gown while Noelle took out the pins at the top that held the bodice in place.

"I'm sorry about what's happened." Noelle stuck the pins in a small cushion. "With the photos and everything. It must be very upsetting for you."

"It was. What he did was so... spiteful. You don't expect someone you love to do something like that to you, do you?"

"Of course not. And I don't think most men realize just how damaging it can be. I don't know your ex, but it wouldn't surprise me if he didn't give a second thought to how it was going to make you feel to see those photos out there. How it might make you feel vulnerable or frightened or violated."

"That's exactly how it felt." Fliss stopped to glance at Noelle. Her throat tightened at the thought that the older woman understood.

"Men don't realize how often we feel unsafe." Noelle slid the straps of the gown over the mannequin's shoulders.

"I hadn't thought of that." Fliss undid the last button, and together they lifted the gown off the mannequin. The beautiful dress was heavy in her hands, full of layers of glittering tulle. Would she ever get to wear something like this? At the moment, she couldn't imagine a time where that might happen.

Noelle hooked it carefully onto a hanger, drew a clear plastic sheath over it, and placed it on the rack. Then she lifted up the one she'd decided to replace it with, and together they began to unwrap it. Ruffles of ivory silk spilled from the bag onto the carpet like cream poured from a carton, glistening in the light. Perhaps she'd take a photo of it once they'd put it up, but that would mean turning on her phone, and she wasn't about to do that.

"It's so weird," she said, "but I've hardly looked at my phone at all since I landed. Back in LA, it was never out of my hand, but here... It's refreshing not to be glued to it all the time."

"I can see why it must be nice to be off the grid for a while. Is it something you're thinking about doing permanently?"

Fliss stopped, her hands in the process of loosening the ribbons on the bodice. "Permanently?"

"Are you thinking of coming out of the business?"

"I'm not sure…"

"Oh, I'm sorry, I didn't mean to imply that you should or anything…"

"No, it's okay." Fliss's heart was racing. "This is going to sound ridiculous, but although I'd fantasized about it, I hadn't even thought it was a real option."

Noelle's cool green eyes surveyed her, and she tucked a strand of her long silver bob behind her ear. "It's always an option."

They exchanged a long glance. Then they returned to getting the gown ready.

"How is your mother?" Noelle asked. "Does she still have red hair?"

Fliss gave a short laugh. "Yes. She refuses to let it go gray."

"Very wise."

"Not at all. I love your hair. It's very…"

"Please don't say distinguished."

Fliss chuckled. "Shiny, I was going to say."

Noelle sighed. "I wish I was the sort of person who believed in growing old disgracefully. I know other women my age who dye their hair and wear outrageous clothes and climb mountains. But I've never been like that. I've always done the right thing."

"Like your son," Fliss said, and smiled.

Noelle gave her a wry look. "I'm guessing you don't mean Elliot."

"He's a cop! I would have thought he was very compliant."

"That's an interesting word. Outwardly, he's very compliant. Inwardly, not so much. He's always been the rebellious one. He's the last person I would've expected to become a police officer. But he's very good at the job."

Fliss held up the hanger as Noelle removed the dress, handling the silk carefully. "Do you think he and Karen will be tying the knot soon? You must be looking forward to your daughters and daughters-in-law coming into the shop, so you can dress them up."

Noelle turned to lift the dress over the mannequin. "I don't know. Karen would marry him tomorrow. Elliot… I'm not so sure. Men do seem to drift into relationships because they can't be bothered to find something better. Not that I'm putting Karen down at all," she said hurriedly.

"Of course not. I understand." Fliss helped her lower the gown, spreading the gorgeous skirt over the mannequin's legs. "At least Phoebe's made a good match."

"Oh yes, Rafe is one in a million. He's crazy about her. And he'll keep her on her toes. Now I just need to find someone new for Dominic."

Fliss glanced at her, unable to stop her face heating. Noelle met her gaze, her lips curving up.

"You're a wicked woman," Fliss scolded, touching the back of her fingers to her cheeks.

"I'm sorry. Roberta told me you and he have been spending some time together."

"I hope you don't think badly of me. I know you must all have been devastated when his wife died."

"It was a very sad time." Noelle began to lace up the front of the gown. "Jo was a good girl, and of course they had my first granddaughter, which is just the best thing." She hesitated, smoothing her hands over the silk. "She was good to Dominic, which, as a mother, I very much appreciated. She was a great mother herself, and she was invaluable to the Church and the wider community in general."

Sensing a *but*, Fliss said nothing, concentrating on arranging the soft folds of the silk skirt.

"But part of me wishes he'd never met her," Noelle said.

Fliss's eyes widened with surprise.

"Oh dear," Noelle said. "Now you're going to think I'm a terrible person."

"Not at all. It must be difficult for you, looking after your family and not being able to talk to your husband about any problems."

Noelle cleared her throat as she played with the ribbons on the bodice. "I do miss him. He was very practical and down-to-earth. He didn't stand much nonsense with what we should or ought to say, think, and feel. He would always cut to the chase."

"I think I would have liked him very much."

Noelle gave her a wistful smile. "He'd have loved you. He liked women who were fun and didn't take themselves too seriously. He would never have said so to Dominic, and please don't say anything to him, but he found Jo a bit... stuffy, I suppose. She didn't have a great sense of humor, and could be a little self-righteous, looking down on others who didn't have the same views as herself."

"Oh, really?"

"We always got on fine, but sometimes I wished Dominic had chosen someone who encouraged him to step out of his comfort zone. That's not to say I'm not extremely proud of him, of course. I love that he's so considerate and thoughtful and helpful. But sometimes... I wish he'd let go a little."

An image came into Fliss's head of the way he'd restrained her and screwed her senseless the night before. "I know what you mean," she said, because she couldn't think of anything else to say.

"You just want your kids to be happy, and I always felt that Jo was too highly strung to be truly happy. Her parents were very strict, and it was important to her to do everything right, and to be seen to be doing everything right. Does that make sense?"

It made perfect sense when she thought of everything that Dominic had told her. "Absolutely."

"None of us is perfect, and I'm glad he picked someone like her rather than a woman who was no good for him at all. I don't know what I'm trying to say, really. Just that he's spent too long being a good boy. And it's time someone led him astray."

"You really are a wicked woman," Fliss said.

Noelle raised her eyebrows. "What?"

"Roberta told you we spent the night together, didn't she?"

"Let's just say that I know Emily stayed at Roberta's, and I saw the big smile on his face this morning and put two and two together."

Fliss shook her head and straightened to look at their creation. "You should be warning me off him. Telling me I'm a loose woman for distracting him from his churchly endeavors."

"Very little could distract Dominic from his churchly endeavors, and that's not what I meant at all. I meant that, in his spare time, he deserves to do something distinctly not churchy."

"Please don't mention the missionary position," Fliss begged, and they both started laughing.

Noelle stood back with her, admiring the model, then turned to give her a smile. "I'm just saying that I'm pleased you two seem to have hit it off. And I'm giving you my blessing for the time you're here, for what it's worth."

"This may surprise you, but it's worth a lot. I'm envious of how supportive you are to your kids. How you want what's best for them, and not what's best for you. It's a very important distinction that I'm not sure most parents understand."

Noelle adjusted the skirt of the dress a little. "Hugh always said we had to be careful not to push our kids to do what *we* wanted. Every parent loves it when their kid is a prefect or head boy or top in a school sports team because it reflects on them. They think that all the other parents and teachers are thinking 'Wow, hasn't that couple done a great job with their child, they must be amazing people.' Of course, we all want the best for our children, but the truth is that, as you say, what's best for them might be staying out of the limelight and enjoying pastimes or activities that aren't as fashionable, shall we say, as some of the others."

"It's the same in the States," Fliss said. "There's huge pressure on children and parents to perform in the classroom and the sports field."

"I think we've done okay." Noelle walked back to her office, Fliss following. "The girls seem happy here with the shop and the café. Elliot loves his job. And I don't know that Dominic could have been anything other than a counselor. He was born to help others, and I'm glad he found a role in the Church that helped him grow into that."

"But you want him to loosen up a bit," Fliss said.

Noelle gave her an impish smile. "Maybe a little. And I think you're the perfect person to help him out."

Chapter Twenty-Two

At just after three, Dominic turned up at the bridal shop with Emily in tow.

Fliss glanced up as he walked in, conscious of her sharp inhale, the way her heart rate increased at the sight of him. That morning, he'd dressed in dark-gray pants and his usual light-gray shirt, which she'd learned marked him out as a deacon when he wore his collar, rather than a priest, who tended to wear black shirts. He'd tossed a long black coat in the back of the car, but now it was raining he'd slipped it on. He had his collar on now, too, ready to venture into the community for his afternoon work. He was obviously well-respected, judging by the way people turned in their seats to greet him as he passed, their faces lighting up when he stopped to pay them attention. He struck an imposing figure, tall and handsome. But all Fliss could think about was how he'd made love to her the night before, his passion overwhelming both of them as they'd tipped into oblivion.

She swallowed hard when he walked up to her behind the counter and winked at her.

"Afternoon," he said.

She cleared her throat. "Hey."

"Had a good day?" His eyes met hers, bright green today, almost dazzling. He was thinking about last night too, she could tell.

"Yes, it was good thanks." Her mouth was talking without being guided, her tongue flopping about in her mouth. Her brain had turned to mush. She wanted to climb over the counter and crush her lips to his, strip off all his clothes, and do him then and there on the tiles.

His lips quirked up, and she realized everything she was thinking must be showing in her eyes.

Dominic glanced to the side and his smile turned wry. Fliss looked over to see Roberta and her mother watching them and smiling, talking quietly.

"Emily, do you want to see the new tiaras we've got in?" Noelle asked. When Emily squealed, she took her hand and let her off into the shop.

Roberta walked up to them. "Thank God I've got buildings insurance," she said.

Dominic raised an eyebrow. "What?"

"You two are clearly about to set light to the place. Get a room, for fuck's sake."

He gave a short laugh, and Fliss grinned.

"Your mother has given permission for us to have an affair," she told him.

"You're kidding me."

"Nope. She practically said so earlier."

Dominic rolled his eyes.

"We're pleased for you," Roberta protested. "You're smiling."

"I don't usually smile?"

"Not permanently. And I've never seen you look at another woman the way you look at Fliss."

Not even your wife. Although she didn't say the words, they hung in the air between them, ominous as a thunderstorm.

Dominic's eyes met Fliss. Not knowing what to say to that, she lowered her gaze, but her face warmed.

"So," Roberta said to her brother. "I guess you've looked at the internet today?"

He nodded slowly. Fliss knew he would have seen her name and the photos splashed across most of the major news channels.

"She doesn't want to go back yet," Roberta said. "Understandably so. She's thinking of staying here until the weekend. Until she leaves, I thought it best that she lies low. Possibly under the protection of the Church."

Fliss's eyes widened. "I can't stay with Dominic," she scolded her friend. "What about Emily, for starters?"

"Already figured that out," Roberta replied cheerfully. "She can come and stay with me for the rest of the week. She'd love that. We'll just say that you've got lots of work, Dom, and Fliss is staying with someone else in town or something. Emily won't care. She just wants to play with my cats."

Fliss looked at Dominic, a refusal hovering on her lips. They'd spent one night together, and that's all she'd meant it to be—a hot, sexy, one-night stand. Even if she took a few more days, she'd be going back to LA eventually. It didn't make sense to spend more time with him. It was a crazy idea.

"What do you think?" he asked her softly.

The refusal died away on her lips as she watched his gaze settle on her mouth. He wanted her again. He was thinking about undressing her, putting his hands and lips on her naked body. Jesus, there was so much she wanted to do with him, to him… a week wasn't anywhere near enough. But it was better than nothing.

Mutely, she nodded.

"Great!" Roberta clapped her hands together. "I'll break the news to Emily now. Monkey!" She walked off into the shop.

Dominic and Fliss stayed where they were, facing each other. People moved around them in the café, and outside the rain beat on the window. She could smell muffins warming in the oven and the rich aroma of coffee, and the scent of Dominic's aftershave, imprinted on her mind after the night before.

"I have to do my rounds now," he said, his voice a little husky. "But I'll be done by six."

"I'll need to get my stuff from Roberta's."

"Go home with her, and I'll pick you up from there."

She nodded, then reached out and touched his collar. "Go do some good."

His lips curved up. "I'd kiss you," he murmured, "but at least two of the customers in the room who are watching us right now go to my church."

"That's fine," she said, amused. "It makes the waiting all the more fun."

"Daddy!" Emily came running into the café. Fliss waited for her to ask why he'd made the decision to let her stay with her aunt, but all she said was, "I'm staying with Roberta! We're going to make real ice cream!"

"Bribery," Roberta whispered to Fliss. "You owe me."

"I do." Fliss slipped an arm around her waist and hugged her.

"Aw." Roberta hugged her back. "You both deserve some happiness. Make the most of him."

I intend to, Fliss thought, releasing her, and watching Dominic walk out of the door. Four whole nights with a sexy preacher. Was she crazy? She'd come here in a blind panic, to get away from the man who'd broken her heart, only to find comfort in the arms of someone else. Dominic made her feel better, which was great in one way, and bad in another. She was using him, and that wasn't fair.

Not that he seemed to mind overmuch.

Well, the deed was done now. She helped the others begin to tidy up the café as they prepared to close at four, wiping tables, washing dishes, her heart hammering all the while.

If this was so wrong, why did it feel so right?

*

She went home with Roberta and Emily, packed up her case, then sat in the kitchen watching them while they made their ice cream, mixing the sweetened condensed milk with the cream and adding crushed cookies and chocolate chips to tubs before pouring the mixture over. Once everything was cleared away, they all sat at the kitchen table and made paper snowflakes until Dominic arrived.

"She's all ready," Roberta said cheerfully, winking at him. "Off you go. We've got things to do here and I'm sure the two of you are going to be very busy."

He glared at her, but she just grinned, and Emily hardly even looked up from gluing glittery stars onto her snowflakes when he kissed the top of her head. He rolled his eyes and said goodbye, and they walked out to the car, Dominic carrying her case, her heart racing.

"You're sure about this?" she asked him.

He put her case in the car, then came around to her side. Glancing over his shoulder, presumably to make sure his daughter wasn't watching, he stepped closer to Fliss, pinning her up against the side of the car.

In answer to her question, he kissed her. His lips moved across hers, slowly, sensually, his tongue probing, his body pressing to hers, and she sighed and gave in, opening her mouth and letting him explore until he finally moved away.

"You could just have said yes," she said.

"That was more fun." He left her to walk around to the driver's side. "Now get in. I'm taking you home to do terrible things to you."

"Ooh, how exciting." She yanked the door open, got in, and buckled herself in super quick, making him laugh.

"You're a woman after my own heart." He put the car in drive and pulled away.

"I've thought about you all day," she said honestly as he turned onto the main road and headed for the town.

"Me too." He glanced at her. "Did you really talk to my mother about me?"

"We got chatting while we were sorting out the wedding gowns. She thinks you need to loosen up."

He laughed. "She could be right."

"Of course she's right. I didn't tell her that you'd already started."

He gave her a mischievous grin. "I'm glad about that."

"I was tempted."

His gaze lingered on her. "Thank you for agreeing to stay with me."

"It was very generous of you to ask me."

"So you're staying here until the weekend?"

"I think so. I need more time to decide what to do, plus Kurt hasn't heard from Whitfield yet. I think they're holding out to see how all this pans out. At the moment, it's not clear whether the public are going to be sympathetic or accusatory. They can turn so quickly. Jack's well liked in Hollywood and he's playing on the fact that I dumped him when something better came along. They've got an interview with a few of my 'friends'," and she put air quotes around the words, "who are women I've hardly said two words to, who are keen to point out that I can be superior and snooty and only look out for myself. So I'm not holding out much hope."

"What will you do if Whitfield withdraws his offer?"

"I don't know." She looked out of the window. "I'm so mixed up at the moment. And part of me is conscious I'm sticking my head in the sand by staying here. I know I need to face up to it all and deal with it. But I can't, not at the moment."

He reached out and covered her hand with his. "Sometimes we need time for the dust to settle. I'm sure that after a few days, the path will become clear."

She remembered his mother asking her if she was going to come out of the business, and what Noelle had said afterward, *It's always an option*. Theoretically, it was. She could turn around and walk away. But was that what she really wanted? To give up the career she'd spent a lifetime building? Especially when she was so close to making it?

She could wait and see what Whitfield said, and make the decision based on whether she was offered the part in his movie. But that felt hypocritical. It would be sour grapes if she didn't get the part and then told herself she didn't want it anyway. She needed to make her mind up now. But her brain felt fogged, her heart confused. She loved her job—she just disliked the world it took place in. She hated the superficiality, and the meanness. She was tired of the bitchiness and the way that you could only advance by climbing on someone else who had fallen.

Looking back at Dominic, her gaze fell on his collar, and her lips curved up.

"What?" he said, catching the look.

"Nothing. What did you get up to this afternoon?"

"Visited a few of my parishioners who are too ill to come to church. Mostly they just wanted to sit and talk. I was able to sort out transport for a couple of them, and one of them had run out of firewood and couldn't afford to buy any, so I arranged for Kaia's stepfather to bring some around."

"That was sweet."

"Yeah, he's a good guy. He has a lot of forest on his land, so he has plenty to spare."

"It must be nice to know you're helping people."

"I guess. I don't think about it, to be honest. It's just what you do."

"No, Dominic, most people don't as a matter of course. It's what *you* do."

He indicated to go around the roundabout and didn't say anything.

"You don't like accepting compliments, do you?" she asked softly.

"It makes me uncomfortable."

"Why?"

"Because I'm nothing special. It's my job."

She didn't reply to that, just smiled, and looked out of the window again.

"It's nearly six thirty," he said. "Would you like to go to dinner?"

"No."

He glanced at her. "You sure? I thought you might be hungry."

She wanted this man so much, food was the last thing on her mind. "We'll eat later."

He held her gaze for a long moment before returning it to the road, heading the car toward his home.

Chapter Twenty-Three

It was raining heavily by the time they pulled up, and they ran from the car into the house, Fliss squealing as she found herself soaked in the short time it took her to cross the drive.

"Jesus. Look at me." She stood in the hallway, dripping onto the tiles. She wore a knee-length white dress that was now transparent in places, and when she pulled the clip from her hair, it hung damply around her face. "I'd forgotten how heavily it can rain up here," she said, wiping beneath her eyes.

Dominic put her case down and just stared at her. She was the most gorgeous creature he'd ever set eyes on. He'd thought about her all day, and he'd kept telling himself that his imagination was running away with him and she couldn't possibly be as beautiful as he remembered. But she was. More so, in fact, in the flimsy dress that clung to her generous breasts, the skin on her face and neck glistening. She looked young and fresh and full of life, and when she glanced up at him, her eyes were filled with laughter and light, making him feel incredibly happy.

He put his hands on her hips, pushed her up against the wall, and crushed his lips to hers.

Fliss gasped, her hands clutching his shirt, but he was hungry for her now, and he swept his tongue into her mouth, pressing his body against hers. Her hands snaked up into his hair, her nails scratching his scalp, and a shiver ran down his back, turning him hard as a rock. She obviously noticed, because she moved her hips against him, murmuring her approval.

Lifting his head, he stared into her eyes. "I want you," he said fiercely, smoothing his hands down her sides to her butt.

"I'm all yours," she whispered back. "Anywhere, any way you want. I've been thinking about you all day. I know it's crazy."

"It is." He kissed her again, his lips moving across her cheek, down her neck. "You've cast some kind of spell on me."

"Abracadabra," she murmured, sighing when he slid his hands up to her breasts and brushed his thumbs across her nipples.

He returned his mouth to hers and ran the tip of his tongue along her bottom lip. "I want to taste you. Can I taste you?"

"Yes," she said breathlessly.

His lips curved up. "I've been imagining this all day," he murmured, kissing her slowly, taking the time to tease her tongue with his. "Wondering what you taste like."

"You're such a wicked man," she said, sighing.

"I am, where you're concerned. I'm going to need a new occupation if you keep leading me astray."

"I'm not doing anything," she insisted. "You've always been like this beneath the surface. I've just let the tiger out of the cage."

He chuckled and kissed down her neck, then over her breasts, and finally dropped to his knees in front of her. "Maybe you're right." He pushed her wet dress up her legs, revealing her slim, tanned thighs. "But you're still the one who's holding the key." Reaching the top, he admired her cream lacy underwear for a moment, then hooked his fingers in the elastic and pulled the panties down her legs. She stepped out of them, and he tossed them aside, then slid her dress up again.

Her skin was silky soft and hairless, such a turn on for a guy who'd only ever seen a woman *au naturel* before. Filled with wonder, he stroked across her bare mound with his thumb, then slipped it down into her folds. They both sighed as he found her already swollen and wet, and he moved her legs a little wider, then bent his head and slid his tongue onto her warm skin.

Fliss moaned and wrapped one leg around him, and he supported her bottom with his hands as he began to explore with his tongue. She tasted sweet and rich, and her sighs and groans only served to turn him on more as he aroused her. Making sure she was steady, he moved one hand beneath her and slid two fingers inside her, stroking gently but firmly as he swept his tongue over her clit and sucked until she was panting and clutching her fingers in his hair. Wanting to take her all the way, he didn't stop, just kept up the rhythm until her body tightened, and then he groaned his approval as she came, clenching around his fingers. Enjoying the way he could feel her muscles pulsing, he swirled his tongue over her clit until she relaxed back against the wall, then rose and caught her in his arms as she began to slide down.

"All my bones have disappeared," she said as he toed off his shoes, then carried her through the house to the living room.

"You taste heavenly," he said, pressing his lips to hers. She complained as she obviously tasted herself, but gave in and let him kiss her, sighing when he placed her on the edge of the dining table and lifted his head.

"Making love with you is heavenly," she said, reaching up to touch his collar. "Literally. You forgot to take it off. Naughty preacher man." He laughed, and she undid it at the back for him, and he tossed it onto the chair. "Now you can sin to your heart's content," she told him.

"I don't think it quite works like that." He tugged up her dress, and she raised her arms so he could lift it over her head.

"Let's pretend it does," she said as he laid the dress over the chair.

"All right." He popped the catch of her bra, drew the straps down her arms, and tossed it aside. Then he leaned over her, his lips just touching hers. "You drive me crazy, you know that?"

She gave a little nod, her eyes dancing. "I like crazy Dominic."

"Good, because I don't think he's going anywhere all the time that you're here." He kissed her, pouring his desire into it, the blood racing through his veins at the sight and feel of her naked beneath him. Her body was so soft, her breasts heavy in his hands, and he kissed down her neck to them and took one of her nipples in his mouth, unable to resist them. They were small and light pink, and had tightened to little buds, as the room was cool.

"Are you cold?" he murmured, flicking his thumb over the end of one. "Would you rather go in the bedroom under the covers?"

She shook her head. "I want you to fuck me here."

His heart skipped a beat, and he stopped and leaned on the edge of the table. She met his gaze, unrepentant.

"Do I shock you?" she asked.

"A little bit," he admitted, his lips curving up.

"You want me to stop?"

His gaze dropped to her lips. He was so hard now, he was almost busting out of his boxers. "No. Does that make me a bad person?"

"Of course not. Sex can be loving, but it's hotter when it's bad." She kissed him, then nipped his bottom lip with her teeth. "I bet there are a lot of things you've never done in bed. The thought of letting you do them all with me is such a turn on."

He closed his eyes, his head spinning. "Jesus."

"He's not going to help you now." She began unbuttoning his shirt, laughing as he shook his head. "I think you want to be shocked. You've been a nice boy for far too long. Time to grow up, Dominic. Let the man out." She pushed the two sides of his shirt apart, then set to work unbuckling his belt and unzipping his trousers. When she'd finally released his erection from his boxers, she let out a long sigh, licked her palm, then took him in hand and began giving him long, firm strokes.

He swelled in her hand, his lips parting in a silent groan, and she kissed him, delving her tongue into his mouth. "Come on, Dominic, take me," she whispered when she moved back. "All the way to heaven and back. I know you want to."

Retrieving his wallet from his pocket, he took out a condom and tossed the wallet aside. He ripped off the wrapper, rolled it on, and then guided the tip of his erection into her folds.

Fliss dropped onto her elbows, her head tipping back, her blonde hair spilling across the table. He smoothed his hands across the pale skin of her body, over her breasts, her waist, her stomach, reveling in the sight and feel of her, and loving how different she was to him, with his hard muscles, tanned skin, and scattering of hair.

"You're like a Greek statue," he said, bending to trace his tongue around a nipple, then sucking it into his mouth. She arched her back and moaned, so he did it to the other one, then returned to the first, switching between the two until she clenched her fingers in his hair and tugged hard.

"Please," she begged, so he straightened and, very slowly, pushed his hips forward. She was so wet and swollen from her previous orgasm that he slid in easily, all the way to the top.

"*Aaahhh.* You feel amazing." He closed his eyes, withdrew until he was almost out of her, then pushed forward again, filling the air with the slick sound of them moving together.

"Mmm... That feels good..." She widened her thighs, allowing him easier access, and he began to move with long thrusts, sliding deeply inside her.

He kissed her for a while, then straightened to look at her, getting as much enjoyment from watching her as they made love. Her face was flushed, her mouth blurred from his kisses, and he adored the way she abandoned herself so freely to him, holding nothing back as she told him how she felt, and sighed and moaned.

He should have taken her into the bedroom, laid her on the soft bed, and spent hours arousing her, but this was so hot, so sexy, and she certainly didn't look as if she regretted it. As desire spiraled through him and he began to move faster, harder, she licked her lips and her eyes sparked with excitement, and she let her elbows slide away and dropped onto her back.

"Ah, yeah," she told him, lifting her arms over her head and stretching out, "come on, fuck me harder, make me come, make me scream your name."

So he did, forgetting to be gentle and polite and considerate, and giving in instead to his baser desires that urged him to take her the way she wanted. He pounded into her, his hips slapping against her thighs, incredibly turned on by her erotic moans. He sucked hard on her nipples and tugged them with his fingers when she begged for more, and then she was coming, crying out as he ground against her, her voice saying his name such a turn on that he couldn't have held back if he'd wanted to. He thrust harder, losing himself in her, until the muscles in his groin tightened, and the climax took him in fierce clenches that left him gasping for air.

When he'd done, he leaned on the table, his hands either side of her waist, and looked down at her with helpless wonder.

"Oh my God," she said, "I haven't come that hard in years. Oh, every single muscle in my body aches."

"I'm sorry."

"Don't apologize, it was fucking amazing."

He laughed and withdrew, then lifted her up and wrapped her in his arms.

"I don't know what you're doing to me," he murmured in her ear, "but I like it."

"I'm glad." She rested her cheek on his chest, her arms around his waist. "I know you don't believe in Fate, but I do believe it was meant to be, our meeting. It's just been so amazing. I'm crazy about you, you mad, sexy preacher."

"And I am about you, you gorgeous girl." He meant every word. Did she know, the way he did, that they were already in trouble? How on earth was he going to let her go at the end of the week?

Well, there was no point in worrying about it now. *Worry is the darkroom in which negatives develop*, his dad had used to say to him, and he'd tried to live by that epithet. They had a few days left together, and he wasn't going to spend them fretting about the end.

"Are you hungry?" he asked her.

"I'm starving. I could eat a horse."

He laughed and released her. "Well, I might have some chicken. That'll have to do for tonight."

She hesitated, and he wondered whether she was about to ask if he wanted to go out for dinner, but then she smiled and said, "Chicken sounds great."

He led her into the kitchen, debating whether he should just take her out, and screw everyone who gossiped about what they were up to. But he wasn't ready for that yet. She couldn't afford to draw attention to herself in case someone recognized her, and he was still wary of broadcasting the fact that he was having an affair. And anyway, he wanted to keep her to himself.

They only had a few days. She'd be able to survive on his cooking until the weekend.

Probably.

Chapter Twenty-Four

"We've got something to ask you," Noelle said.

Fliss smiled. Wednesday had been a quiet day in the shop, but Thursday had proven busy, and during the lunchtime rush she'd been helping Noelle, assisting several customers as they tried on dresses and shopped for accessories. Finally, it had quietened down, and they were sitting having a cup of coffee that Roberta had brought them while a woman who was probably in her forties and her best friend giggled like teenagers as they browsed the gowns.

Bianca and Phoebe had joined them, and Bianca had just elbowed Phoebe, who'd then elbowed their mother, prompting her to ask the question.

"Ask away," Fliss said.

"On Thursdays, we stay open late for our evening fashion show," Noelle said. "They're usually fairly well attended."

"Yes, Roberta told me about them," Fliss replied. "You have some local girls in to model the gowns, don't you?"

"That's right. Unfortunately, though, the two girls who usually model are in Auckland this week. So… we wondered whether you'd like to help out tonight?"

"And model the gowns?"

"Yes. Just for fun. Of course, feel free to say no. It's not everyone's cup of tea, and—"

"I'd love to," Fliss said immediately. "Be a princess for a night? Why on earth would I turn down that opportunity?"

"Fantastic!" Bianca clapped her hands. "It's going to be such fun!"

"Have you seen any dresses you'd like to model?" Phoebe asked.

"Actually…" Fliss rose, went over to the racks, and lifted off one of the gowns. It was one of Phoebe and Bianca's, with an elaborately beaded bodice and a skirt that fell to the floor in folds of gorgeous cream satin. "This is so beautiful it makes me want to cry."

"It's one of my favorites," Phoebe said with a smile. "You should totally wear it. It will really suit you."

Fliss held it against her and stood in front of the mirror, turning to admire the dress. "I should make the most of modelling it," she said absently. "I'm not sure if I'll ever get the chance to wear one of these for real."

She was almost talking to herself, and when she glanced at the others and saw the look on their faces, she waved a dismissive hand. "I'm sorry, I didn't mean to sound so self-pitying."

"That's okay," Noelle said. "God knows you have a reason to feel like that after what you've been through."

"Even so. I know how lucky I am to be in this position. It's not everyone who gets the chance to be a movie star." She'd meant to sound genuine, but even she could hear the note of bitterness in her voice.

"Have you heard from Mike Whitfield yet?" Phoebe asked as Fliss put the dress back on the rail.

Fliss shook her head and sat down again. "I spoke to my agent this morning. I think everyone's waiting to see which way public opinion is going to swing."

"I read an article yesterday that was very complimentary to you," Phoebe said helpfully. "I wasn't gawking," she added, "I was trying to help…"

"Thank you." Fliss swallowed down an unexpected lump in her throat. These women didn't really know her at all, but they were on her side. It was a humbling thought, made somewhat bittersweet by the fact that while the friend who had caught Jack kissing had called her to say she was glad she'd got shot of him, she hadn't been particularly sympathetic about what he'd done with the photos. Her sisters hadn't called, no doubt jealous of all the attention she was getting. Her mother was still angry that she hadn't yet returned to LA, and she'd been exceptionally cutting that morning when Fliss had phoned her after speaking to her agent, stating flatly that she was surprised Fliss was such a coward.

"Do you think I'm being cowardly?" she asked Noelle and her daughters. "By hiding here, I mean, and not getting out there and dealing with it."

"Not at all," Noelle said immediately. "Of course not. The kind of person who'd revel in this sort of attention must be very self-centered. Just because you're an actress, it doesn't make you narcissistic."

"I'm surprised you're out at all," Bianca said. "I'd be in bed with the duvet over my head crying my eyes out. I think you're really brave."

"Aw, thank you." Fliss was touched by their response. "I do feel like that, and nobody in the business seems to understand. They all think I should be enjoying the limelight. But I feel as if I'm standing in the middle of an airport or a railway station and I've stripped off and everyone's staring at me. And that's not how I want to live my life."

"Of course not," Phoebe said. "Especially when it's your ex who's forced it on you. What a bastard. I think I'd have shot him for that."

"I've been trying to rise above it. I don't want to sink to his level and start a public slanging match. But it's getting harder. I see what the news sites are saying about me, about how I dumped him because I thought I could do better, and I think Jesus, if only they knew."

"I'm not surprised he's jealous," Bianca said. "The role in Whitfield's movie would be quite a coup, wouldn't it?"

"It's sure to catapult me from the B list to the A list," Fliss replied. "I'd hopefully get some more great parts off the back of it. If I get it, and I'm not sure I will now." She cleared her throat. "Anyway, Dominic will be here soon, so I'd better help Roberta tidy up."

"You two seem to be getting on well," Phoebe said innocently. Bianca kicked her. Noelle just smiled.

Fliss blushed. "We are. He's a good guy."

"One of the best," Phoebe said. "He's been down for a long time, what with Jo and then Dad. It's good to see him letting go a bit."

Fliss thought about the last few days. They'd spent the evenings together, most of the time in bed, making love, talking, eating, then making love again. Last night, he'd awoken her in the early hours with soft kisses along her back. She'd lain in the dark, half asleep, while he stroked her breasts and between her legs until she'd sighed with desire. Then he'd rolled her onto her front, slid inside her, and thrust slowly until they both reached a lazy, sleepy climax.

"I think he is," she said, rising, not missing Bianca's smirk. "See you gals later."

She walked off, conscious of the whispers behind her, knowing they were all thrilled at her burgeoning relationship with their brother. It made her smile, but as she started to collect plates and mugs from the tables, her smile faded, and she felt despondency sweep over her. She couldn't bury her head in the sand forever. In just a few days she was going to have to return to the real world and stop the fantasy she'd been indulging in. All she was doing here was playing another part, pretending she was a preacher's girlfriend, respectable and liked in the community, when the truth was that they hadn't been seen together, other than at the fair, because Dominic was undoubtedly too worried about what his parishioners would think.

He was a good man who'd been loyal to the memory of his wife, and she'd tempted him away from his principles and forced him to indulge in an affair that he was bound to regret once she left.

She felt a sweep of shame. She'd slept with him to make herself feel better. She'd used him, and he deserved so much more than that.

The front door jangled, and she looked up to see him enter, Emily skipping ahead to run up to her aunt. He was wearing his collar and looked smart in his gray shirt and dark trousers, his hair damp from the light rain. Wow, he was such a handsome guy, and nice with it too, a pillar of the community, trustworthy, honest, and kind.

She really was going to hell.

*

At seven p.m., Dominic dropped her back at the bridal shop for the evening show. They'd spent the previous few hours in bed, with him pulling her back every time she'd tried to rise, telling her he wanted to make the most of her while he had her.

Fliss's mouth was tender from his kisses, her muscles aching from the three orgasms he'd given her, and she would have preferred to crash out in front of the TV rather than spend the next two hours parading around in front of an audience. But as she walked into the shop, she smiled to see the café packed with customers, sipping wine, and eating canapés, and the Goldsmith girls dashing about, getting ready for the show. Phoebe was already in one dress, ready to model it to the watching crowd. Emily, who as a special treat was allowed to be there for the evening, sat under Roberta's watchful eye.

"This way," Noelle said as Fliss took off her coat, leading her into the changing rooms. "I've put the gown you liked on the peg—I hope I've got the size right. I'll help arrange it once you've got it on."

"Thanks." Fliss closed the door and studied the beautiful dress with a sigh. At least she could pretend to be a bride for the evening. It wasn't all bad.

She took off her clothes, then carefully removed the gown from the hanger. Outside, someone had started playing music, and she could hear Roberta talking to the audience, introducing the evening, and then cheers as Phoebe must have walked out in her dress.

After stepping carefully into the gown, Fliss pulled it up and slipped the straps over her shoulders. Oh… it was beautiful, the satin cool, heavy, and rich, the bodice glittering in the light. She opened the door and stepped out to admire herself in the mirror, blinking away tears at the sight of herself looking like a princess.

"Oh, you look amazing," Noelle said. She zipped her up carefully, then spent a moment rearranging the skirts. "It's not too tight?"

"It's perfect," Fliss whispered. "Exactly what I would have chosen." She bit her bottom lip to stop it trembling.

"Aw." Noelle rubbed her arm. "Are you okay?"

"I was just thinking how a girl is supposed to do this with her mother."

"You've got plenty of time," Noelle soothed. "You're not even thirty yet."

Fliss nodded, too tired to explain that she couldn't imagine ever wanting to go through this with her mother. Annabel Rivers had always put her own feelings and wishes before her daughters'. Fliss had spent most of her life searching for her mother's approval, and never getting it. She'd always made excuses for Annabel's behavior, telling herself that her mother had her best interests at heart, and that was why she pushed her daughter so much, and why she could be so harsh, if not cruel. But after what had happened with Jack, Fliss was no longer sure that was the case. Annabel wanted Fliss to be a movie star so she could live vicariously off her fame and bask in the reflected glory, just the way Dominic had said that parents pushed their children to be prefects so that other parents would look at them and think what a good job they'd done.

Why had she put up with it for so long? Always feeling as if she wasn't doing enough and was letting her mother down. Why did she give Annabel so much power over her?

She was done, she thought, as she turned in a circle, feeling the skirt billow out. Done letting other people tell her what to do. Done letting others make her feel that the decisions she made were wrong because they didn't fit their vision for her.

In fact, she was just done.

She stopped turning, the skirt falling softly around her legs.

She was done.

She loved acting. But she hated LA, she hated most of the people in the business, and she hated the lifestyle. She'd let others convince her that the only way to be happy was to become more and more famous, and that settling for less than that meant she'd failed. But they were wrong.

Had Roberta failed because she's opened her own café and spent her free time cooking and working in her vegetable garden?

Had Phoebe failed because she'd turned her back on the offer to work in a huge bridal store and had instead decided to stay in her family's bridal shop and do the thing she loved most in the world?

Had Dominic failed because he'd chosen to stay in the town he adored and do his best for those who needed his help, rather than traveling to other countries to try to save the world?

Of course not. She had one chance at life, and it didn't make sense to spend it trying to please other people.

Her decision wasn't connected to Dominic, or at least, not directly. She had no idea what she was going to do yet, or where she was going to live. Maybe she'd return to Wellington or Auckland and pick up a role in a Kiwi movie. Or maybe she'd do something else. Whatever, she was done with LA, and she'd tell her agent that Whitfield didn't have to make a decision anymore—she didn't want the role.

"Are you okay?" Noelle asked.

Fliss turned and put her arms around the older woman, giving her a big hug. Noelle laughed and hugged her back.

"Thank you so much," Fliss said, her voice husky with emotion. "I so appreciate everything you've done for me over the past week."

"I haven't done anything." Noelle patted her soothingly.

"You have. More than you know." Fliss moved back and kissed her cheek. "Your girls are very lucky."

"That's sweet." Noelle blushed. "Thank you."

Phoebe entered the changing rooms, her face glowing. "Oh, that was fun! Are you ready, Fliss?"

"Yes, sure." She slipped her feet into a pair of shoes that Noelle had laid out for her, then walked out and down the long room toward the archway that led to the café. The audience cheered as she approached, and she laughed and gave a twirl, loving the way the beads on the dress caught the light like camera flashes.

Who needed a red carpet at the Oscars when she could be the star of the show here?

Chapter Twenty-Five

"What's this I hear about a party tonight?" Fliss asked Dominic.

It was late, or maybe early, depending on your point of view, just before two a.m., and they hadn't yet gotten to sleep. She'd had a lovely evening, prancing around in various gowns, and then when Dominic had picked her up and taken her home, he'd pressed himself up against her as soon as he'd closed the door, insisting that he'd missed her and had thought about her the whole time.

Fliss hadn't argued when he'd carried her off to bed, happy to spend hours kissing and touching him, and talking about their evening. Plus—and she had to admit it to herself—she liked the way he looked at her while he touched her, as if he adored her, and she was the most beautiful thing he'd ever seen.

She was tired, and she'd have to make him go to sleep soon because he needed to get up in about five hours, but she smiled as his lips curved up when she mentioned the party.

"I didn't think you'd want to go," he said. "An eighties revival? I couldn't imagine it being your sort of thing."

"It's totally my sort of thing! Roberta said she'd help me with an outfit."

He grinned. "You really want to go?"

"I do." She hesitated. "We don't have to go together, if that's worrying you."

He frowned. "It's not."

"Honestly, it's okay. I know I'm not exactly preacher girlfriend material, and that's fine."

He pulled her closer and cupped her face. "Hey. I accept that I'm a bit nervous about announcing to everyone that I'm having a fling, but it's nothing to do with you being acceptable 'girlfriend material'. I don't want people looking at you and pointing fingers. You deserve your privacy. And what we have here is private. I don't want people asking questions. I wouldn't know what to answer anyway. I don't want to have to analyze this and compartmentalize it. Other people will say it's just about sex, and…" He pursed his lips. "Okay, I know there's been a lot of sex…"

She chuckled. "Just a bit."

He looked into her eyes, and his smile faded away. "But it's more than that. For me, anyway. You've brought a light to my life that hasn't been there for years."

"It *is* more than that." She turned her head and kissed his palm. "Of course it is. We're not the sort of people who can sleep with someone and forget them the next day. It has to be meaningful for us to open up like this."

They studied each other for a long moment. It was dark, just a little moonlight to coat the room in silver, and quiet too, not a sound outside, even the owls having gone to sleep. It was as if they were the only two people in the country awake.

"I'm leaving LA," she said.

Dominic's eyebrows rose. "What?"

"I decided earlier. I've spent too long doing what other people want without thinking of myself. I like acting, but I don't want fame and fortune. Not like this. I've been so unhappy. Why do I keep putting myself through it? I'm done with trying to please Kurt and my mother. I don't want to do it anymore. I'm going to move back to New Zealand."

He looked completely stunned, his jaw dropping, words failing to spill out.

"I'm not doing it because of you," she said. "Not directly. I'm not expecting anything. I might continue acting, I'm not sure yet. I might do something else. I'm excited at the thought. I don't know where I'll live, Wellington, Auckland, I'm not sure. But you've helped me to see what it is I really want."

"What is that?" he asked softly.

"To be happy. To do a job that brings me joy. To go home at night and not have the world peeking through my window. To help people, maybe. And to find someone to share my life with who'll love me for who I am and not who they want me to be." She lifted his hand to her lips and kissed his fingers. "I'll have to go to LA one more time to finalize everything. But when I come back… I'd like to see you again.

Even if it's only as friends. I like you, and I trust you, and I don't want to lose that."

A smile spread slowly across his face. "I'd like that."

"You're sure?"

He gave a short laugh and rolled onto his back, pulling her with him. "Of course I'm sure. I know we can't predict the future based on a few nights together, but I think it's obvious that I'm crazy about you. Isn't it? Or do I have to show you again?"

"You need to get some sleep," she scolded, happier than she'd been for weeks, months, maybe even years.

"Sleep, shmeep," he said, and proceeded to show her just how crazy about her he was.

*

The superintendent of the local police station and his wife had been married for thirty years, and they'd decided to celebrate by inviting half the town to a party at their house. When Dominic pulled up and parked half a mile away on the already crowded drive, he saw streams of people walking toward the house with crazy hair and outrageous clothes, carrying bottles of drink and plates of food to contribute to the buffet.

Smiling, he made his way to the house, stopping to talk to everyone on the way, and by the time he arrived, the rest of his family were already there, the guys drinking beer and rolling their eyes at the costumes, watching the girls as they danced to Wham's *Wake Me Up Before You Go Go*.

"Hey," he said, walking up to them, grinning at the sight of Elliot dressed as Adam Ant with a military jacket and a white stripe painted across his nose and cheeks. "Nice outfit."

Elliot ran his gaze down him, taking in his plain black clothes, clerical collar, and electric-blue hair and frowned, then started laughing. "Don't tell me," he said. "Deacon Blue."

"Right first time." Dominic accepted a beer from Rafe and chuckled at his outfit. Rafe wore skin-tight jeans, a white T-shirt, and checked braces, with a pork-pie hat.

"I kinda like it," Rafe said. "I might keep it."

"I know what you mean." Angus's rolled-up denim dungarees and checked scarf made him look as if he'd stepped out of Dexy's Midnight Runners. "This is really comfortable."

"Mind you," Rafe said, "I think the girls have disowned us. Phoebe's not talked to me all night."

Dominic grinned and looked across at them all dancing with Emily. Roberta was done up as Madonna, complete with pointy boobs, Phoebe looked like Debbie Harry, Bianca wore a floaty dress and had fluffed up her hair to make her look like Kate Bush, and Fliss... At first, he couldn't see her and frowned as he searched the crowd, and then he realized. His smile spread. She was wearing a wild auburn wig, an off-the-shoulder top, bright eye makeup, and fingerless gloves, and looked just like Cyndi Lauper.

He walked up to her. "Hello, gorgeous."

"Hello, you." She laughed and reached out to touch his hair. "Deacon Blue! I love it!"

"I hope that's a temporary color," Roberta called out. "Otherwise your parishioners are going to be in for a shock tomorrow."

"Aren't they all temporary?" He feigned shock, then grinned as he caught hold of Fliss's hand and spun her in a circle. "You look amazing."

"I haven't had this much fun in ages." She gasped as he pulled her toward him and she met his chest with a bump, and then she put her arms around his neck and hugged him. "Thank you so much for rescuing me."

"What do you mean?" he asked, conscious of a couple of his parishioners glancing over at them.

"You've taught me what's important in life. I can never thank you enough."

"I'm sure I can think of a way," he murmured into her ear, and she laughed and spun away, her eyes alight.

He watched her return to the other girls, his heart racing a little. When she'd told him she was going to move back to New Zealand, his mind had spun so fast he'd felt dizzy. He'd spent all week trying to force his brain to understand that their relationship was only temporary, and all of a sudden she'd implied they might have a future. He could hardly believe it. At that moment, he had no idea how it would work. All he cared about was that she wanted to see him again, and the promise of a future with her was enough to keep him happy for the moment.

*

They danced and ate and drank and laughed for hours, and it was only when it started to get cold and the moon was high in the sky that Roberta carried a sleepy Emily back to her car, and everyone started to make a move for home.

Dominic kissed the women and shook hands with the guys, said goodbye to a few other people he knew, and then headed back to the car with Fliss.

"Are you sure you don't mind being seen with me getting into your car?" she asked as they walked up and he unlocked it.

In answer, he pushed her up against the passenger door and kissed her, taking his time, enjoying the feel of her lips against his, one hand creeping onto her butt as he cupped her head with the other. Her wig came off in his hand, and she laughed as he spread her hair around her shoulders, then kissed her again.

It was only when car lights flashed on them as someone drove past that they broke apart, laughing.

"All right," she said softly, "I believe you."

"You'd better," he said, going around to the other side. "Because I'm mad about you, and I'm this close to shouting it to the whole world."

Chapter Twenty-Six

Fliss smiled at the customer as she finished serving her, and then blew out a long breath. It had been a busy Saturday morning, and even with Libby and Angie in the café, all four of them were run off their feet.

Nevertheless, she'd worked with a spring in her step, buoyed up by the conversation she'd had with Dominic the night before. He wanted to continue to see her, and although both of them were old enough not to be fooled into thinking this was love yet, she couldn't stop her stomach flipping at the thought of a possible future with him. To be with a man she could trust, who would never betray her, seemed more than a dream come true.

So even though she'd booked her flight for tomorrow, and she was a little nervous about returning to the fray, she knew she was coming home, and that was enough to keep her going.

"Coffee?" Roberta asked her, and she nodded and sat at a nearby table, putting her feet up on a chair. "You are crazy," Roberta said as she started steaming the milk. "You could have sat at home for a week and just read or done crosswords. You didn't have to work."

"I like working. I wanted to spend time with you all. And I've made lots of new friends." Fliss smiled at Libby making sandwiches behind her, and she grinned and waved.

At that moment, her phone beeped in her pocket, announcing the arrival of a text. Fliss pulled it out, discovering it was from Kurt, and she read it without thinking. It was short and sweet.

Amazing news! Whitfield wants you! You're going to be a star!

Her heart shuddered to a stop. Her head spun.

She had the part?

The door jangled, announcing a new customer, and she looked across in a daze. It was a young man. He stood in the doorway, his gaze scanning the room, saw her, and walked across to her, holding up his phone, presumably recording the scene. "Felicity Rivers?" he asked.

She stared at him, her mind still spinning. "Who are you?"

"Simon Trent, Northland News."

Her jaw dropped. He'd discovered that she'd got the part in the movie already? Talk about good news traveling fast!

Trent adjusted the angle of his phone. "I understand you've been staying in Kerikeri undercover. Have you seen the photos of yourself on the News?"

Now she was confused. "What photos?" she asked before she could think better of it, her heart pounding.

"What's going on?" Roberta demanded at the look on her face. She came around the counter and glared at the reporter.

Trent ignored her, still training his phone on Fliss. "Of you and the lucky Reverend Goldsmith. How long have you two been seeing each other? Have you set a date yet?"

A sliver of fear slid down Fliss's back. "What?" she whispered, completely confused.

"Get out," Roberta said to him, "before I punch your fucking teeth down your throat."

"I've got every right to be here," Trent snapped. "The public have a right to be informed on events and opinions."

"Don't quote the fucking journalist declaration at me. Get out!" Roberta pushed him, and he stumbled and backed away to the door. The few customers in the shop stared at them, and Fliss saw one of them holding up her phone to take a picture.

Roberta closed the door on Trent and locked it, then ran through to the shop and locked the door there too. "We've got a problem," she called to Noelle. Coming back in, she announced firmly to everyone, "I'm very sorry, the café is closed."

Grumbling, the customers left, one of them taking photos all the way. Trent was outside, holding his phone up to the window. As they watched, a woman walked up to talk to him, and behind her were two men, one carrying a proper TV camera, one with sound equipment.

"Fuck." Roberta took Fliss's hand and marched her through the shop.

"What's going on?" Noelle asked, alarmed, as Phoebe and Bianca came out to see what the fuss was about.

"The press has discovered that Fliss is here." Roberta took her into Noelle's office, which only had one window that looked out onto a small fenced yard at the back.

Shaking, Fliss sank onto the chair. "Something's happened," she said. "The reporter mentioned Dominic."

"You must have been seen with him." Noelle turned her computer screen to face them all. Quickly, she brought up the Northland News's website.

On the front page was the headline, *Found her! And you'll never guess!* Beneath it was a handful of pictures that told the story.

There was Fliss, walking across the domain on her own, and there again, snapped with Dominic at the school fair. There were several photos of the two of them together, and then one of them caught in a kiss, which must have been taken after the party the night before. Fliss remembered thinking she'd seen a flash of car lights and realized it must have been a camera flash. They looked good together, she thought absently, spotting the way his hand had slid to her butt and tightened possessively.

The last photo was of her right there, in the bridal shop, in the wedding gown she'd modelled, twirling and laughing, looking as if she'd won a million dollars.

"When is the big day?" the news site asked. "And what will Jack Leeson think of it all?"

Fliss didn't care about Jack, or her fans, or the reporters, or what anyone in LA would think of it all.

But she did care about Dominic, and his family and friends. Emily was going to see this, and so was the rest of the community. There would be a scandal—exactly what Dominic didn't want. It made their love affair seem sordid and tacky, and it wasn't. What she felt for him was rare and beautiful, like one of the pearls that Phoebe had sewn onto the gown she'd worn. And now it was ruined.

Putting her face in her hands, she burst into tears.

"Oh dear," Noelle said.

"I'm ringing Dominic." Roberta walked away, putting her phone to her ear.

"I'm calling Elliot," Phoebe said. "There are going to be more reporters once word gets out."

"I think we should get her out of the shop," Bianca said.

"Where?"

"Back to Roberta's place?"

"They'll find her there."

"Well now they know she's up here, they'll find her wherever she is, probably."

The conversation continued on around her as they called and talked and tried to organize, but Fliss knew it was out of their control. Once the press got its hands on a story, it became a living, breathing thing, like a feral dog, and there would be no bringing it to heel.

"Hey." Noelle dropped to her haunches beside her, pushed a tissue into her hands, and rubbed her back. "Come on, it's not the end of the world."

"I didn't want this for him," Fliss whispered, and blew her nose.

"I know."

"I'm so sorry." More tears poured down her cheeks. "I'm sorry that Emily's going to find out."

"Oh goodness, my granddaughter's going to be excited as a girl with two heads to find out that her dad's been dating you. She worships the ground you walk on."

"That's very kind of you," Fliss said with a hiccup, "but I don't think Dominic will feel the same way. He didn't want her to know. He'll be cross that it's all come out."

"Dominic doesn't do cross," Noelle said. "He'll be fine."

But Fliss didn't think so. He'd made it clear that he wanted to keep their affair quiet, and she couldn't imagine why he wouldn't be angry. Maybe not at her, but he was bound to feel frustrated and wish that he hadn't met her.

"Jesus," Bianca said, peering around the doorway. "There's a crowd out there now."

"Everyone's wondering what the fuss is about," Noelle said. "Can you see any more reporters?"

"The crew have set up. Looks like they're filming the front of the shop. There are a couple of people trying to take photos through the window."

"Elliot will be along soon," Phoebe said, appearing around the corner. "He might be able to clear the pavement."

"I don't know that he can force journalists away from a public road," Bianca stated, "as long as they're not blocking pedestrians."

"He'll do his best," Libby said. "You know what he's like."

"I should go." Fliss wiped her face. "You've had to shut your shop, so now it's interfering with your business. It's not right." She should go back to LA, take the part in the movie, and put this all down to experience, a dream that was never meant to be reality. Her heart sank at the thought, but she had no choice.

"You stay right where you are." Noelle had a glint in her eye. "You're not to blame for any of this. We'll sort it out. I'm going to make you a cup of coffee, and then we'll have a chat and decide what's the best thing to do."

Voices rose outside, and Fliss looked up in alarm. "What's going on?"

"Dominic's here," Angie called from the café. "Shall I let him in? Oh, Elliot's here too."

Roberta ran out, and Fliss pushed herself to her feet, wiping her face. She didn't want to see Dominic right now. If he was angry, she didn't think she'd be able to cope.

"Is there a back way out?" she asked Noelle.

The older woman just rubbed her arm, listening to the commotion outside. The door opened, and Elliot could be heard yelling to everyone to get back. Then the door closed again.

"Fucking idiots," Elliot said, adding, "Sorry," to someone. Oh no, they hadn't brought Emily, had they?

Fliss heard the two men walking through the shop, and she bit her lip and held her breath.

And then there was Dominic, stopping in the doorway to the office. His gaze fell on her, his green eyes bright. There was no sign of anger on his face. Only quiet amusement.

"You're supposed to let me propose before you buy the dress," he said.

Fliss covered her mouth with her hand and burst into tears again.

"Aw." He walked forward and put his arms around her. "Come on. It's not that bad."

"I'm sorry." She sobbed into his shirt. "I didn't want anyone to find out."

"It was only a matter of time before someone put two and two together. And made fifteen, obviously."

"I shouldn't have modelled the dress. It was a stupid mistake. I shouldn't have—"

"Stop it," he said, firmly this time, moving back from her a little so he could look at her. "You've done absolutely nothing wrong."

She glanced down to see his daughter standing to one side, watching them. Fliss went over to the little girl and took her hands in her own. "I'm so sorry about this."

Emily's cheeks went red. "I think it might have been my fault."

Fliss glanced at Dominic, who said, "What do you mean?"

"I told Kaia what you told me about Fliss being an actress. And I think she told her brother, who told their uncle, who works at the newspaper." Her bottom lip trembled. "I'm sorry. I didn't mean for this to happen."

Fliss dropped to her knees in front of the girl and took her in her arms. "It's okay, it wasn't your fault. It wasn't anybody's fault except mine."

Emily hugged her. "I'm sorry your boyfriend was horrible to you and posted those photos on the internet."

"Me too."

"Are you and Daddy getting married?"

Dominic chuckled, and Fliss blushed. "No, sweetie," she said. "The journalist saw me modeling a dress and made the wrong assumption. But I do like your dad, a lot."

"I'm glad." Emily let her go. "He's been so happy since you came here."

Fliss looked up at him. His lips quirked up and he tipped his head from side to side as if to say *Yeah, she's right.*

"He makes me happy, too," she whispered.

"All right. Enough of the soppy stuff." Elliot, strikingly handsome in his police officer's uniform, walked into the office. "We should be able to sneak you out of the back entrance to the car, and we'll get you to Roberta's. We can't guarantee that they won't find you there, but you're flying out tomorrow, anyway, right?"

Fliss nodded, touched when the faces of everyone around her fell. "I'm coming back though," she said.

Roberta stared at her. "What?"

She took a deep breath. "I'm leaving LA and coming home. I don't know what I'm going to do yet. But I do know that I don't want to be an actress anymore. I'm not sure I ever did."

Roberta flung her arms around her. "Come and live with me!"

Fliss laughed. "That's very sweet."

"I mean it! Live with me until you sort out what you want to do, and come and work in the café. You've seen how busy it gets and we're desperate for help."

"I… I'll think about it," Fliss said sincerely, glancing at Dominic. "But thank you so much for the offer."

Dominic's eyes were full of joy, and his face was one big smile. "Elliot's right," he said. "Let's get you to the house, and then we can all talk about where we go from here."

*

There was no point in opening up the shop again, so everyone went around to Roberta's, and there ended up being a kind of party atmosphere, especially once Fliss agreed to Roberta's plan.

It would be the perfect temporary solution, she thought to herself as she wandered down to the bedroom she'd slept in a few times before staying with Dominic. She needed time. Time to decide what she wanted to do with herself. Time to let the phenomenon that was Felicity Rivers die down, and to let the real Fliss Rivers shine through. And time to let her relationship with Dominic progress at a natural rate. She wanted to date him properly, and for them both to make a decision about their future based on how they felt, rather than feeling they were forced into it by circumstances.

"Having second thoughts?"

She turned to see Dominic leaning against the doorjamb. Even though she'd literally been talking to him a few minutes ago, she didn't miss how her heart skipped a beat at the sight of him.

"No," she whispered, leaning back against the windowsill as he came into the room.

He lifted a hand and cupped her face. "Are you sure? You could always do this movie with Whitfield and see how you felt afterward. I appreciate it's a huge opportunity."

"I've never felt more certain of anything in my life. I feel so happy right now, Dominic, I can't tell you. And so much of that has to do with you." Tears stung her eyes. "I was so worried that you'd be angry when you realized the town was going to find out about us."

"I don't do angry."

She gave a short laugh. "That's what your mother said."

"Why would I be angry? I've been seeing the most beautiful actress in the whole of Hollywood. My street cred has gone up by a thousand percent."

"Your street cred?"

"It was zero to start with."

She chuckled, and he wrapped his arms around her.

"You're not worried about what your parishioners will think?" she murmured. "Or your bishop?"

"This is New Zealand, and the twenty-first century. Ultimately, love is all that matters."

"Love?"

He rested his lips on the top of her head. "I know that love is something that develops over time, and I don't want to rush things. But I fell in love with you the moment I saw you."

"Covered in mud?"

"Covered in mud. And I've only fallen further since that moment."

"My fallen angel?" she whispered.

"I don't think what's going through my mind could be classed as remotely angelic." He slid his arms down to her butt and pulled her against him.

"I'm sorry I've corrupted you," she said, wrapping her arms around his neck.

"Are you really?"

"No." And she kissed him, her heart filled with joy.

Chapter Twenty-Seven

Two weeks later

Dominic leaned on the gate surrounding the small arrivals lounge and closed his eyes against the warm autumn sun.

It was the last flight of the day, and the airport was moderately busy. A man with a camera who Dominic was pretty sure was a reporter stood on the other side of the lounge, but Dominic ignored him, concentrating instead on the small plane as it passed overhead and touched down on the long runway.

"Do you think she'll be hungry?" Emily said, jumping up and down by his side.

"I'm sure she'll be ravenous," he told her.

Emily grinned at him. She'd made chocolate brownies with Roberta that morning, especially for Fliss, and she couldn't wait for her to taste them.

The plane turned and headed back down the runway. Dominic's stomach did a flip, and his heart started to race.

"Are you going to kiss her?" Emily asked.

He looked down at her. "Do you think I should?"

"Oh yes! Girls like kisses."

"How do you know that?"

"Dad…"

"I don't want you kissing boys until you're at least thirty-five."

"Dad!"

He laughed and pulled her to his side. "Come here." He kissed the top of her head. "What would I do without you, eh?"

"You'd be useless."

"I would."

"You can always ask me for advice about girls, Dad."

"I do need it, it's true." He smiled as the plane turned in front of the airport and came to a stop. His heart lifted. At last. He'd missed her so much it hurt.

She was one of the first out, and he watched her walk down the steps, his heart thundering. She wore beige slacks and a cream sweater, and he felt a twinge of pride when the reporter took a few photos of her approaching the lounge at the thought that this beauty was his.

Almost. He was working on it.

She came through the gate, then stopped and laughed as Emily ran up to her and threw her arms around her waist. "Hello sweetie! I've missed you!"

"I'm so glad you came back," Emily said.

"Me too." Fliss's gaze met his, and her eyes lit up as he approached. "Hey, you," she whispered.

"Hey." He slid an arm around her shoulders and lowered his lips to hers, not caring that the reporter was capturing the kiss. "Mmm." He lifted his head and squeezed her. "It's been too long."

"I spoke to you this morning," she teased, moving out of the way so the guy could bring in the trolley with all the bags. "And every other morning and evening since I've been away. And in the night, sometimes." Her eyes twinkled. Dominic had called her only a couple of nights ago to tell her how much he missed her and what he was going to do to her when she got back, which had turned them both on so much they'd ended up having phone sex.

"It wasn't enough," he said simply. Listening to her sexy sighs had been amazing, but it didn't hold a torch to having her in his arms.

"I know." She cupped his face, her turquoise eyes suddenly serious. "I can't believe how much I've missed you."

"You're sure?" He'd tried not to panic when she'd gone away, but he had to admit that a small piece of him had feared that she'd realize her feelings weren't that strong while they were apart.

"You once told me I was like a flower in a city," she said.

"A touch of beauty amongst the concrete and steel. I remember."

"Well that's how you are to me, too. Amongst all the pretension, the insincerity, the fake tans, the painted faces, coiffured hair… All I could think about was coming home to you. I don't think you realize, Dominic, your honesty and your faith shine through you and resonate like a bell, clean and pure."

"What I'm thinking now is neither clean nor pure," he murmured in her ear, and she laughed and swatted him.

"Behave when I'm trying to be deep and meaningful." She spotted her bag and moved to lift it down.

"I'll get it." He retrieved it and carried it outside for her, back to the car, Emily skipping by his side.

"Did you see the reporter?" he asked Fliss as they walked.

"I did. Just the one. I'm already old news." She'd announced her retirement from Hollywood a few days after returning to LA, and Dominic had watched her deal elegantly and competently with the fallout. For a whole week, she'd sat for interviews and related the story of how she was tired of acting and wanted to return home. She'd talked about Jack and the photos and had done her best to explain to the world how it had made her feel vulnerable and unsafe. As soon as she'd spoken up, public opinion had swung violently in her favor, and it was Jack now who'd been forced into hiding to get away from the accusatory press. Rumor was he'd have trouble ever getting another part. She'd told Dominic she was sorry it had to end that way, but everything that was happening to Jack he'd brought on himself.

For the last few days, things had been quieter. No doubt the public would glance at a photo of them kissing and smile, but he had the feeling it wouldn't be long before she was right and she'd be yesterday's news.

They all got in the car and Dominic headed off for Roberta's house, which was only ten minutes from the airport. "Everyone's coming around later," he said. "They all want to toast your return."

"I can't wait to see them. I've missed them all so much."

Dominic felt a warm glow of pleasure at the thought that she'd missed his family and friends. He was glad she had people who were supportive and loving toward her. The rest of the people in her life had been decidedly unhelpful. Her agent had yelled at her down the phone when she'd turned down Whitfield's role. Her mother hadn't spoken to her since she'd announced she was giving up acting. Neither of her sisters had even bothered to call her.

As they drew up outside Roberta's house, his sister came running out, and as soon as Fliss was out of the car, Roberta wrapped her in a big hug.

"I'm so pleased you're staying with me," Roberta whispered furiously. "It's going to be such fun!"

"I've really missed you!" Fliss hugged her back. "Thank you so much for asking me to stay. I know how precious your peaceful house is to you."

"Meh. It can be lonely, too, sometimes. It'll be nice to share it with someone for a change."

"Come on," Emily said, tugging Fliss's hand. "I'll pull your case to your room for you."

Fliss laughed. "Come on, then," she said, and then two of them headed off to her bedroom, Fliss casting Dominic a smile over her shoulder before she disappeared.

Dominic gave his sister a wry smile, and the two of them walked into the house, through the living room, and out onto the sun-filled deck where Roberta was in the process of sifting through some knitting patterns that were spread over the table.

"Pleased to have her back?" Roberta asked, starting to gather up the patterns.

He gave a nonchalant shrug, then grinned.

"You've been like a bear with a sore head without her," Roberta scoffed.

"Have not."

"Yes, you have. I'm guessing I'll be looking after Emily every other night from now on?"

He gave her a rueful smile. "It's not the ideal arrangement, I know."

"I'm happy to do it. I adore my niece. We have the same mental age of fifteen." Roberta grinned and placed a bunch of patterns back in the bag. "But why don't you just ask Fliss to move in with you?"

He hesitated. "I thought about it. But firstly, I don't want to rush things. I want to give her time to settle and work out what she wants from life."

"Fair enough. Even though I think she already knows what she wants. But you said firstly; what's secondly?"

"I do have to think about my job. The bishop's happy to turn a blind eye to a discreet relationship, but living with someone is another matter."

"I guess." Her green eyes looked up at him with a touch of admiration, which surprised him. "I'm sorry for teasing you in the past about the decisions you've made. I can't say I've always understood them, and I've been frustrated mainly because I've felt that it's held you back sometimes. But I do admire the way you stick to your principles."

"Stop it," he said. "You're making me blush."

"I mean it. I just want you to be happy."

They both turned and watched as Emily brought the plate of chocolate brownies and put it on the living room coffee table, and Fliss joined her, sitting on the sofa and taking one of the brownies as Emily offered it to her. She took a bite and said, "Mmm, they're delicious," smiling as Emily beamed.

Roberta gestured with her head for Dominic to follow her down the garden a little, out of earshot. "What are you going to do about Fliss if you can't ask her to move in with you?"

He stopped and glanced across at the beautiful woman who was chatting away to his daughter. "I'm going to ask her to marry me."

Roberta stared at him, her jaw dropping.

"What?" He looked back at his sister, his lips curving up. "Not yet, obviously. I'll bide my time and wait until she's ready. But I know she's the one for me."

Roberta's eyes filled with tears. "Oh my God, you just completely took my breath away."

He laughed and wrapped his arms around her. "You old softie."

"I wish I could find someone as sweet as you," she whispered, sniffing.

"Oh, he's out there," Dominic said. "I've never been more certain of anything in my life. How could any man fail to fall for you?"

"Quite easily so far," she mumbled.

Dominic laughed. "Have faith, sweetheart. Keep your heart open, and love will find a way in." He kissed her forehead. "Now come on, those brownies smell amazing, and I'm starving."

Epilogue

Two months later

The cool evening air fluttered the leaves on the vines, but Fliss didn't notice it at all. Mac, the owner of the Blue Penguin Bay vineyard, had placed several heaters around the large deck, and so even though she only wore the beautiful satin gown she'd modelled in the Bay of Islands Brides Shop, she barely noticed the fact that it was nearly midwinter.

"Not cold?" Dominic asked, pulling her closer into his arms anyway. They were dancing, just the two of them, while their friends and family sat inside, talking and laughing and watching them with smiles on their faces.

"Not at all." She linked her fingers behind his neck and smiled up into his green eyes.

"And you're not regretting marrying me yet?" he asked softly.

She chuckled and reached up to kiss him. "Of course not, silly. I'm just amazed we waited as long as we did."

It had taken Dominic almost exactly four weeks of living apart before he'd relented and asked Fliss to marry him. She'd known it was coming, because there wasn't really any other way they could be together, and it had been obvious to both of them that even though they insisted they wanted the other to be sure, neither of them wanted to wait.

Touched that he loved her enough to want to marry again, Fliss hadn't hesitated to accept his proposal, and after that they'd both decided there was no point in waiting six months or a year to make it official. They'd said their vows at his church just a month later in a quiet ceremony attended only by his family and their friends, with Emily finally getting to wear the gorgeous bridesmaid's dress she'd wanted for so long.

Fliss had asked her mother and sisters to come, but her mother had refused, and her sisters had both declared they were too busy. She couldn't deny that had hurt her feelings, but she had a new family now, which was more than a lot of people had, so she was determined not to get too upset over the loss.

The press had managed to get a few photos of them together, and no doubt they were running the story now with headlines about their whirlwind romance, but Fliss didn't care. All that mattered to her was that tomorrow she was moving into Dominic's house for real, and it would be the first day of the rest of their lives.

And now they were at the vineyard just down from the town of Russell, run by a friend of Roberta's. Winifred, known as Fred, was an English girl who'd inherited the vineyard when her father died. She'd married the guy who was running the estate to gain her inheritance and had promptly fallen in love with him. Fliss and Dominic had decided to have a party there after the wedding, and they were all staying the night there.

They'd talked about what kind of honeymoon they wanted, and when Fliss had suggested what had been brewing in her mind, Dominic had agreed with a laugh that it sounded like great fun. So the following weekend, a large group of them were all flying out to Las Vegas for a few nights. Roberta was coming, and Phoebe and Rafe, Bianca, Angus, Elliot and Karen, and Libby and Mike, and it promised to be a huge laugh. Much to her disappointment, Emily was staying home with Noelle.

"It's been a wonderful day," Fliss told her husband, happier than she thought she'd ever been in her whole life.

"The best," he said.

"I once told you I was only looking for comfort, and that I wasn't expecting true love and a ring on my finger," she said. "I can't believe I have all those things."

"I know what you mean. I walked into the house that first day we met without any knowledge of what was coming. And when we were talking that evening, I just kept thinking wow, this woman is amazing, why hasn't anyone snapped her up?"

"And now *you've* snapped me up," she said, lifting her face to his.

He kissed her lips. "I have indeed." He took her left hand from behind his neck and showed her the ring on her finger. "And this tells any other guy who might be interested that you're mine."

Her lips curved up. "You like that, don't you?"

"I do."

"Mr. Possessive."

"Yep."

"Mmm. I might escape, though."

"True. Maybe I need to tie you up so you can't get away."

Fliss shivered, and he chuckled and kissed her again. Inside the restaurant, everyone cheered, and they laughed and turned to wave.

"Let's have a last glass of champagne," Dominic said, "and then I think it might be time for bed."

"It's only nine o'clock," she scolded him.

"It's also my wedding night, so I hope you got a good night's sleep last night, because you won't be getting much tonight."

Laughing, she led him back into the restaurant, where they proceeded to dance the night away with the people they loved.

Newsletter

If you'd like to be informed when my next book is available, you can sign up for my mailing list on my website, http://www.serenitywoodsromance.com

I also send exclusive short stories and sometimes free books!

About the Author

Serenity Woods lives in the sub-tropical Northland of New Zealand with her wonderful husband and gorgeous teenage son. She writes hot and sultry contemporary romances. She would much rather immerse herself in reading or writing romance than do the dusting and ironing, which is why it's not a great idea to pop round if you have any allergies.

Website: http://www.serenitywoodsromance.com
Facebook: http://www.facebook.com/serenitywoodsromance
Twitter: https://twitter.com/Serenity_Woods

Printed in Great Britain
by Amazon